triumph
OF THE APE

I0552609

stories by Todd Dills

Many of these stories' early versions were published in the following magazines or anthologies between the years of 2000 and 2010: *Red Mountain Review*, *Lumpen*, Featherproof's mini-books series, *Chicago Noir*, *Hair Trigger*, *Knee Jerk*, *Kiss Machine*, *Holiday in Cambodia*, and *THE2NDHAND*. The author wholeheartedly thanks the editors and publishers.

THE2NDHAND | Nashville, Tenn. | the2ndhand.com
ISBN-10: 0983465843
ISBN-13: 978-0-9834658-4-3
Library of Congress Control Number: 2012923616

Cover illustration by Andrew Davis

A tremendous collection! *Triumph of the Ape* outlines the highs and lows of comically self-conscious young men bumming around the free world, armed only with mind, heart and humor. These stories are bursting with warmth and smart lovin'. Reading Todd Dills makes life—all of it—feel a little bit kinder.
                —**Patrick Somerville**, author of *This Bright River*, *The Universe in Miniature in Miniature*, *The Cradle*

Triumph is dauntless, daring in its variety of tones and styles, a kind of taunt to the new century and all its ongoing crises. There's the spirited, Southern slant of the Barry-Hannah-esque "Color of Magic" and "Confederate Yankee…," and elsewhere, the author's ongoing interest in forms shifts toward the collection's centerpiece, an imagining of an underground literary movement centered around a "Stupidist Manifesto." Realism, noir, short short—from lascivious to hilarious—the range of styles culminates with one-part music essay, one-part end-of-days fabulism, in the closing sound track to a coming Rapture. Again and again, there's invention, Dills' inexhaustible gift for language and tireless imagination.
                —**Joe Meno**, author of *Office Girl*, *The Great Perhaps*, *Hairstyles of the Damned*

Every story in *Triumph of the Ape* reveals characters "united in stupidity, not necessarily dumb or incapable of love but senseless with self-love," typical of Dills' weirdly entertaining Faulkner-in-the-city touches. Perhaps no other working writer has so benefited from living in two very distinct environments, first the South, then years in Chicago, then back to the South, with countless time spent on the road to here, there and everywhere. Dills deals in lore for apes triumphant in the downfall. He once again proves himself a master of tradition gone haywire in a country addicted to its own mythology, supplying the antidote with his 21st-century folklore.
                —**Paul A. Toth**, author of *Airplane Novel*

I met Todd Dills some years ago at a cult-hero party fueled by drink and ethical drugs. He was anonymously disturbing, and was adjective-impaired, for a literary icon. In retrospect, he was wearing a fictional suit. He catapulted pretty much everyone, tossing people at the city like darts. People were afraid, all those years ago. And now Todd has written a book.
                —*Rumpus* 24-hour professional book blurber **Mickey Hess**, author of *The Nostalgia Echo*

For the memory of Josh Shenton

With special thanks to my wonderful wife, Susannah Felts, and Eric Graf, C.T. Ballentine, Joe Meno, Liz and co. at Quimby's Books, Jacob Knabb, Anja Kirschner, Randy Albers and the rest of the Columbia College FWD, Andrew Davis, Joe Jarvis, Marc Mayfield, Jim Munroe, Jonathan Messinger, Zach Dodson, Rob Funderburk, Chuck at East Side Story, Mickey and Danielle Hess, brother Jeff, my folks and that guy at the Rock Hill, S.C., Waffle House with the Ric Flair hair.

TRIUMPH OF THE APE

Most blues are subtitled either
"No Sense of Wonder"
Or "No Sense of Scale"
—David Grubbs

★ the color of magic. ★

WHEN we got to Vicksburg, Willy and Juanita weren't back from the barbecue joint and their faux gate was locked tight. We parked in the driveway just beyond it and walked around its edges to the house. I lit a cigarette. Corky, my wife, scowled, dropping her bag on top of a patch of poison ivy that snaked its way over an unused section of driveway onto the front steps. I made a mental note never to touch the bag again, then looked down and realized I was standing on a vine myself.

"This place is overgrown," I said.

"I can't see anything," she said.

"Watch out for the poison ivy," I said. "It's dark."

"No shit."

I didn't know what we were doing here—there was work to be done in Birmingham, where we lived, work to be done in Tuscaloosa, where my office was. I had become numb. Silly way to begin, I know, but it was true. I was spending an hour on the highway every day before and after work, where I sat in front of a computer, talked on the phone, typed. I knew what I was doing, I was pretty good at it, instinctively—the work simply didn't afford the opportunity for much true thinking about life, purpose, meaning, etc., as it was being done.

I am at least well compensated for the useless task.

The people on the phone ranged in intelligence from out-right imbecility to some of the brightest of our nation, wasting their lives as federal government functionaries. If you've never talked to one of them, I assure you: Agency-level functionaries may be occasionally browbeaten by their pigheaded superiors into something like stupidity, but if happen you get one on the phone, ask him or her about a recent book or play or whatever you like.

Earlier in the week I was elated by a conversation with a public affairs officer at Alcohol, Tobacco and Firearms, a woman named Nancy. She thought it was the propensity for and momentous quality of narrative reality, that moment when a reader, reading a book, suddenly cried at the death or silent humiliation of a character, that gave writing its ultimate power—identification, the power of words strung together to elicit feeling from even the garden variety of humanity. In the case of the high-toned experimentalists among our literary giants, like Faulkner, she said, "the real power always comes back to the same things—heaven in the moment, in your chair, at home, tears streaming down your face."

It was a beautiful conversation, the fact that I brought to it something quite different neither here nor there.

But then Nancy threw me by bringing up Terry Pratchett's roman-fleuve *The Colour of Magic*. Sublime narrative reality is the last thing the pop sci-fi satirist brought to my mind. I ended the conversation quickly, sadly, and cosmically trudged off to my blank place, that magical haze-gaze into the distance between the tip of my nose and the computer screen.

It's lonely for an intellectual in Alabama. Hell, it's lonely here for most anyone, I guess, unless you get off on hunting wild pigs.

AMID the poison ivy on Willy and Juanita's steps, I began to tell Corky about my conversation with ATF public affairs officer Nancy Seldy, but before I could get through it she huffed, turned her head away from me, eyes shot out into the dark where the driveway disappeared up by the road, to our car, and she asked me for a cigarette. "Really?" I said. She hated smoking, and often seemed to reserve a special disgust for the people who did it, myself included.

"Yes," she said. "If you're gonna tell me about your stupid conversation with your D.C. girlfriend, I figure chemical stimulation would help me get through."

The organization I worked for had an office in Tuscaloosa in a flophouse you'd figure some student lived in if you passed it—a bungalow from the 1930s or '40s with a vermin-infested basement and fire ants in the backyard and just a sole occupier nine to five—me. I spent a great deal of the time in the backyard, actually, mind intent on the work of the ants, whose tireless devotion to their home-building bespoke a dedication unmatched among the human race. I didn't know anything like it, anyway. We didn't have these bugs up north, of course, not even in Carbondale. Last time I inquired of the National Academy of Sciences they hadn't even made it as far north as Columbia, Tennessee, south of Nashville. They swarmed after a rain at certain times of the year like termites. They attacked sticks I occasionally jabbed into their mounds. My job was to observe, I thought during these backyard sojourns, observe and learn. I knew jack shit about homebuilding, after all.

My real job? I've probably said too much already, but it dealt with the *F* part of *ATF*—I was a strange bird on the streets of Tuscaloosa. I dressed more college kid than marketing/research functionary, spinner of information, but I was obviously too old to be among the first group. The young blondes didn't pay me a second of attention, the more ubiquitous fat boys and girls both might wonder about my social classification for half a second before wandering back into their death stars of self-hate, their own blank magic places the color of the University of Alabama T-shirts they inevitably wore, the deep red of dried blood, gore.

The precious few occasions I had to venture to the police department or the site of a shooting in the region, I might get a haircut and put on a button-up.

CORKY was less than appreciative of the finer points of everyday life. Small things were of no use. Flowers meant nothing to her. Books she might not appreciate unless they were of the old-historical approach, her personal obsession, the past a vast tapestry to be forever woven into perfection, the grand protests of the more scholarly informed of her students be damned. She was the age of the new yet of the old school, I guess. She taught at the university in Birmingham, but she should've been a columnist for the *New York Times*, I told her. I have said it many times.

I gave her the cigarette, and we chain-puffed like the steel mills in Gary on Lake Michigan.

There would be no further word exchanged between the two of us before the headlights of Willy and Juanita's ancient VW Rabbit, some 20 minutes later, gave illumination to the clouds of smoke around us.

They brought the barbecue in, cold. "We got held up in the Exxon," Juanita explained. "Not literally like at gunpoint or anything. See, they've got this new brand of coffee there."

"It's the same shit they've always had," Willy proclaimed—he drank from his cup, on which was emblazoned the nom de guerre "Extreme Javanian." When the big, bearded man swallowed, he made a face. "Goddamn filth. Putting it in a pump dispenser with a bunch of damned colors on it don't make it no better. Can't nobody make a cup of coffee right around here."

Willy then quietly brandished a stove-top espresso maker and began to fill it with water.

"It's named different, though," Juanita said, "and Willy here had to point it out to the pimply clerk."

"It — is — a — goddamn — swindle," Willy articulated.

I laughed. We'd known the couple at Southern Illinois in Carbondale, near as foreign a territory to us as the Mississippi wilds we sat in now. The difference between Chicago and Carbondale is more than just a foot or more of snow each winter, after all.

"Y'all still wanting to go to the military park?" Juanita said. She'd started in on the tub of slaw that came with the barbecue order. None of us had yet had a bite. "The *Cairo* sunk out here. One of them old ironclads. Funny old story—Confederates invented the water mine, I think, which they blew up the *Cairo* with."

"I'm from Cairo, you know," my wife said. Juanita did indeed know Corky hailed from the town, way down at the southern tip of Illinois, or should have at least remembered it, but she just smiled dumbly. Just like a damn Southerner.

"Gimme that goddamn slaw tub," Willy said. The coffee was done, and we both sipped the strong brew—very good, by Mississippi standards. Hell, any standard.

"Here here," I said, raising my cup, and moved with him toward the kitchen table as the women talked on.

Corky knew more about the history than any of us, of course, more than she would initially let on. I braced myself for the lesson as we ate, and it duly came.

The *Cairo* crew was comprised of a significant number of my wife's ancestors, she said, a man particularly she could trace to her mother's family, and its building was undertaken by Union soldiers in Mound City, Ill., just up the Ohio River from Cairo, part of six ironclads on which rested hopes of Confederate defeat. Eventually, the men charged with the boat's operation did their duty, but the *Cairo* didn't make it that far— the first to go down, she died in an accident attributable to hubris, Corky said, hubris evidenced in the ruddy complexion you could deduce from the old black-and-white photographs of the face of the man commanding the flotilla (Thomas O. Something that sounded like "Suffrage" for all I could make out through my chewing) that brought her into the Yazoo channel near Vicksburg on a waterborne raid, where she met her demise, the first boat sunk by an electrically detonated water mine anywhere in the world, according to Corky.

"This shit's pretty good, ain't it?" said Willy. I nodded, though obviously Willy didn't know from barbecue.

"Extreme," I said, scooping shredded pork into my mouth. "Extreme Javanian pig."

"That's the name of that coffee," Willy said.

I smiled, shrugged. "Just a joke," I said.

"Huh," he said. He chewed.

"Yeah, not very funny, I know."

WHEN you read these words, this story, I want you to remember the time, wherever you happen to be—the concurrent events—like you would the occasion of hearing a good song for the first time, maybe an old song, some of that early Metallica or something slightly more recent, Steve Albini's prog-punk Shellac or the Jesus Lizard or even something once as obscure as the young Ian Williams, late of Don Caballero or Storm & Stress, the jazz drumming of the latter, the loop-de-loop electric guitar of the former delivering a pyrotechnic flavor with the instrument otherwise unseen in this world and calling to my mind Chicago 1998, snowstorm New Year's Eve blowing in with the sadness and brutality of a 17-hour drive from down South. Cold, pissing in the Lafayette-area rest stop on I-65, old Dixie Highway, my way back home to crowded drunken apartment parties, dim conversations in dusty barrooms.

It's my fault we moved, it is. My job brought us south. On the rare occasion I hear that wild-ass Mexican polka from some guy's smoke-spewing VW Rabbit I remember our former life, a dream of nightly camaraderie, always a fresh face and a new mind to get our own heads going. Lots of drinking, too, little accountability for much of anything. Or, rather, *responsibility*—very little of that. I loved it. But then I deal with loneliness differently than most—I don't take it out on myself, I guess. Corky misses it all even more than me, and I've always suspected that she acquiesced to the move because to her small-town mind Birmingham, Alabama, sounds like a more proper place to raise a child than mean-streets Chicago. Not that we ever talked about that.

WILLY has seen a UFO. After the women went off to bed, he took me outside and shined a flashlight on a spot off in the darkness among the trees, poisonous ivy snaking up them.

"Right goddamn there," he said.

"Cool," I said.

The UFO looked like a beetle, he said. "With big antennae all lit up blue and golden. Real neon, like at the beach on the boardwalk."

"Magic," I said. "Did it speak to you?"

"'You — don't — believe — in — us'," he said, all mock-gravitas. "You don't believe me, do you?"

I could only shrug. Willy wasn't dumb or crazy, just unsculpted by the hands of polite Southern society. Which wasn't at all a bad thing, I just hadn't figured him for UFO sightings.

"That's OK," he said. "It was right there, though," pointing again into the trees with his flashlight. I looked hard at the spot—I imagined a leprechaun, green, of course, perched on one of the smaller tree's lower branches and picking off poison ivy leaves, rubbing them carelessly across a devilish smile. "Only the beetle knows where the pot of gold goes," I said, quite in spite of myself. Willy frowned, cut his light, and deliberately turned round back toward his front door. I thought, care of a YouTube-distributed satirical news segment that made the rounds that St. Patrick's Day, *Could well be a crackhead playing the part, that time in Chicago outside Lounge Ax, the twenty-somethings with their cocaine confidence and silver shoes crushing my sober teenage heart.*

"I ain't afraid," I said to Willy's back.

"Good," he said, turning round. "That's how they get you." He moved toward me. "Listen, I'll tell you a secret I'm not sure you know already. It's fear that blinds you."

"To UFOs," I said.

"No," Willy said. He stared hard at me. "Not just that. Everything, the goddamn truth. They tell you to cut your hair, they mean to make you fear the consequences if you don't—death, dismemberment. That's the way down here, man. There's a reason everybody owns a goddamn gun."

"No arguments there," I said. I could feel it coursing through me.

"Now let's have us a drink," Willy said.

OR it could be NYC, September 11, 2001. A beautifully clear day in Chicago, too, and I don't know about you but I was listening to heavy metal when I first caught sight of the towers burning on the TV screen. My memory is less of the relentless drinking bout me and Corky and some others had that afternoon than the megalopolis 15 hours by car to the east itself, my friend walking his dog—BOOM.

I can thank the television. I'd been away from TV for years at the time, so I was particularly susceptible to the box's charm. Metallica raining down from a smoke-filled sky.

But I ended the day with jazz. Chicago jazz, sound track to back-porch-fire-escape camaraderie at the top of a three-floor walk-up, view of the Sears Tower, cigarettes' the only smoke in the sky. Safety. The satin ecstasy of winter on its way.

Dawn in Vicksburg, I watched Corky scratching at her left forearm in her sleep.

"You didn't touch your bag, did you?" I said.

She murmured. *Scratch scratch.* She looked like she was mad, lips pursed. I couldn't remember going to sleep.

"What did I do?" I said. Willy'd talked about his UFO, miniature Chinese men appearing in the narrative, for another hour and a half over whiskeys. "Long night," I said.

She still didn't respond.

What would the community think about two grown men drinking into the wee hours while their wives slept? Not much, I figured.

"You smoked a cigarette in this room," Corky said, waking.

"I did not." But as if in the throes of muscle memory a strange déjà vu took hold of my body. I leaned out over the edge of the bed to find a cigarette stubbed out on the old wooden floor.

"Juanita didn't like it," Corky said, sitting up. *Scratch scratch.* I laid back down. Shit. Corky grabbed my foot and started laughing in her sleepy way. She then pounded the ankle playfully on the bed. "I want a baby," she said.

I wrenched my foot away from her grasp—it immediately started itching. *Scratch scratch.*

"You're not going to answer, per usual," she said. She didn't bring it up often. She jumped up and huffed off into the bathroom. I scratched and scratched and scratched.

"I'M sorry I smoked upstairs, Juanita," I said at breakfast—sausage, eggs, pancakes, syrup, lots of syrup.

"What are you talking about?" she said. "You can smoke anywhere you like."

"You don't want me to go outside?"

"No."

Corky snickered.

"I'm just kidding, honey," said Juanita, smiling wanly. "Go outside."

When I finished eating—Juanita and Corky were still nibbling, Willy'd been done for ten minutes or more—I began making the motions of opening a fresh pack of smokes and got through the whole crackling cellophane production, had even popped one in my mouth before the women burst into laughter. I looked at Willy and he shrugged. "I don't know what the hell's so funny," he said. "Go on and smoke."

So I did. I lit it, anyway. Then walked out the front door.

Willy followed.

"They got any UFOs at the military park?" I said, laughing a little.

"They got ghosts," he said. He didn't laugh.

"You were serious about that UFO."

Willy stared at me. "What makes you think I'm joking about the ghosts?" His eyebrows shot high.

I smiled, smoked.

"Gimme one of them cigarettes," Willy said.

We smoked.

VICKSBURG is all dobro and harmonica, acoustic guitar picked by an overfed white dude trying to sound like Robert Johnson but moving way too fast. Think of a sweltering summer outside the windows of your little cartoon four-cylinder in the Vicksburg National Military Park next time you hear something resembling that strain, whether it's the real thing or the poor facsimile and whether you've been there or not. Remember this.

Plastered across the front page of the newspaper today was a story about a morbidly obese woman killed by her policeman lover. She'd rotted considerably, the newspaper said, though they put it in a different, even more insidious way, referring to her flesh as "necrotized."

"Goddamn sick," Willy said, as Juanita read the words aloud from the backseat of the car.

"Now if that ain't fear-inspiring black and blue," I said, turning to Willy and winking. He didn't laugh.

We were coming upon the melodramatic statue of Brigadier General Lloyd Tilghman, who is depicted atop a small hill holding the reins of his spooked horse with one hand and brandishing his sword high in the air with the other. General Tilghman was killed in the decisive battle of Champion Hill here on these grounds, and Willy attempted in his way to conjure a vision of the battle in our brains, gesturing dramatically across the long rolls of the lines from the Confederate positions here through trees to where we'd been when we got here, on the other side of the forest, Union lines. General John Logan was on the other side. Logan—the namesake of the old Chicago neighborhood where Corky and I spent two years before Birmingham, before Vicksburg.

Willy stood just right of the Tilghman statue and mimicked the man's raised sword with his left arm, voice booming out across the green expanse. "Here you have the grand clash of civilizations, your own grand clash!" Willy roared, turning to us and pointing. "You might think of it that way. Now we all know how it came out the first time—God save the Union— but the future of the new clash is unknown."

The ceremoniousness of the whole thing was laughable, surely, but neither Corky nor Juanita was laughing. Corky looked like she was frightened by the man's gravity. I shook my head and chuckled a bit, looking off into a stand of bushes behind the Tilghman statue for an escape route, a place to piss—we'd been out here for nearly two hours and the Extreme Javanian we'd picked up on the way was ready to return to the earth. When I finally looked back at Willy he was staring at me. "Whether you choose to take up the charge, young man," his voice booming into the trees and my brain, "will be your choice and the key to your destiny. Yours alone." Willy's face was red with what appeared to be genuine passion, his eyes in a magic place just beyond my right shoulder. I couldn't help but laugh, thinking all the while of Nancy's comments on sublimity, on potential intensity of experience, the color of magic. Willy was writing it as he went along. I suspected he'd gotten stoned somewhere along the way and was too stingy to share.

"I've gotta piss," I said.

"Soldier on, young man, soldier on," Willy said.

Juanita walked up to where her husband stood and placed her hand on his left shoulder, bringing that raised arm down and proceeding to lead him back toward the car.

Corky and I went back into the bushes, through them on a well-beaten path that led to an old cemetery built along a now-disused road. Corky yelped and went careening over an old ironwork fence into the graves. I parked myself in front of a thorny bush and unzipped, pouring a steady stream into the roots. I closed my eyes.

Just as I finished, a felt a sharp sting on my ankle, then another, then another. I looked down to find my left foot planted firmly in a low fire-ant mound—much smaller, this one, than those in the backyard of my Tuscaloosa office, but big enough. I hopped back and jerked off my tennis shoe, flung it as if to get it well clear of the mound, only to have it hit a tree and bounce back square onto the mound. My shorts fell down in the process, and by the time I had them back up and zipped my poor shoe was being destroyed by the ants as if a sentient intruder itself. I suppose it was.

I sat down on the grass and Corky called out to me. I didn't have the heart to respond. The fire ants were killing my shoe. I examined my ankle—four little red dots where I'd been bitten—and cursed myself for not pulling up my black socks, for taking Corky's sage advice to push them down, for giving in to that pressure to not stick out, to blend.

Maybe the fear was getting to my lovely, crazy wife—the Southern manner, the very essence of the people's being, as Willy explained it. Politesse at its most basic, outright hood-winking fakery at its worst, it was based on fear, and it'd worked its way into her bones.

Or perhaps not.

She came over, finally. I didn't look up at her. "Goddamnit," she said. "They're fucking it up for real."

"Scary, huh," I said.

"No, just…" Corky grabbing the back of neck and turning my head to her. I looked back at the shoe, a straight streaming line of ants winding along the length of one of the laces' ends and coming back around the other side.

"Do you want to raise kids in a place like this?" I said.

"We haven't even started trying," she reminded me.

They'd been at it for five minutes or more. "I wonder if Willy knows how long they'll be," I said. "In Tuscaloosa they usually give up on a stick in a minute or so."

"Maybe it's your stink," she said, still behind me, her voice low. I looked back and up at her. She was unbuttoning her shorts. "C'mon," she said. "I want a baby."

We did it erect against the hip-high ironwork, faces poised over the grave of Stella, Aug 12, 1874 to July 26, 1942, and Arthur Reid, Aug 8, 1874 to Feb 27, 1961. The dates looked like they had been scrawled into the gravestone with a stick.

When it was done I came to retrieve my shoe, and it was clean. Willy was asleep in the backseat of the cartoon car—Juanita was smoking a joint next to him. "Have fun?" she said.

"Yeah," Corky said. She got in and drove us on out of the park—it was Chicago that blared from an oldies station the opening trombone strains of "Does Anybody Really Know What Time It Is?" but I couldn't recall the name at the time. Didn't particularly matter, it was one of those moments you'll never forget, that tune, as Corky began to sing along—loud, fearless—her voice cutting through the smoke wafting up from the backseat, the very color of magic.

week above the umbrella.

19 FEB | I am looking for the Skunk Ape. I saw a film this evening in a dirty rock 'n' roll bar in which the protagonist, a young punk in a punk rock band, is set upon by the Skunk Ape, southwestern Florida's answer to Bigfoot. I know of the creature from old lore and, generally, reading too many books. The main problem with the film was that, as stated by the filmmakers, the majority was shot on location in, well, Chicago.

I want the Skunk Ape to be real, I do—his location should not matter. But the flaw was palpable and unfortunate as regards my quest. This I did not tell the filmmakers, anyhow, nor the lady I'd run into beforehand, at another bar. We got a little drunk and, as I was leaving, she said to me, "You know, I do like you, I think." Like she was trying to convince herself.

"So the truth comes out," I said.

"I am a drunk," she said, much more convincingly. And then she kissed me.

I did not resist—participated, in fact. "You like me," she said when it was done.

"I do." I did, truly, but sometimes the day-to-day intrudes on one's ultimate wishes.

"OK," she said as she wobbled away. "I'll see you."

20 FEB | Lady does not remember kissing at all. This does not surprise me. I could only vaguely recall it myself, waking, head pounding, calling in to work and heading fast off to sleep once more. I got a call from her midafternoon or so and she was asking me how she got home. I had absolutely no idea, I said. A friend told her that she'd been making out with him as well, or so it appears, in addition to a few others. She had no particular memory of this, either. "So what do you got?" she said. I told her. She didn't seem surprised.

I sent an email to Brent Van Nawsea of the *Naples Daily News*, of Naples, Fla. His name sounds as if native to my ears, Cherokee or some such, but he is a confessed Ohioan journalist living in Floridian exile, likewise a staunch anti-Skunk Ape activist, a vitriolic, though occasionally stupid and sappy, columnist whose diatribes against the creature reflect the deep-seated nature of his hatred.

He is a non-believer.

"Brent," my email read, "How dare you, sir—how dare you, indeed—in the face of indisputable evidence to the affirmative, deny the reality of one of God's creatures. Are you the Devil? You should be burned at the stake. Cordially yours…" etc.

A friend suggested we head to Toronto, where Frenchman Alain Robert, who climbs skyscrapers freehanded and illegally, was rumored to be in town surveying the CN Tower, if not making a climb.

It was all over the Internet, my friend said. "There's your Skunk Ape," he said. When Robert climbed the Sears Tower in 1999 I stood out in the August humidity on Jackson by the river, from a distance watching as his small form inched up the massive slick side of the building, disappearing into the cloud cover amid a roar from the other onlookers at ground level. Skunk Ape indeed, without the massive chest and hairy body but surely with the stink, being French.

I have decided that we will go.

21 FEB | I should be jaunting southward in my search, south toward the bed of my curdled upbringing, the land of God-haters and -lovers and -fearers and buttermilk, fried chicken and fried turkey and fried pickles and chicken-fried steak and everything. At work—work like a good habit, something I am not much given to, truthfully—I was almost surprised to receive a response from a thoroughly nonplussed, and eagerly surly, Brent Van Nawsea.

"It seems someone's got a case of the …," wrote the columnist.

He actually typed the "…".

"I do not know what your problem is, sir, but if you ever come down here to my office from wherever you are I'll show you a thing or two about what a length of time living in Florida will do to a man's temper. Cordially…"

Seems Van Nawsea stands by his story about Mr. Jimmy Semper, owner of Swamp Lake Campground in Ochopee, Fla., the only Skunk Ape promoter in the world outside the international cult of cryptozoologists—and other than myself, of course, and those filmmakers, who made a complete travesty of mine and Semper's search for the truth.

Van Nawsea condemns Semper for making a mockery of his state.

But Semper is a believer. Never mind the fact that every time he sights the Skunk Ape his campground is undergoing a financial crisis.

Semper claims to have sat for two hours every day in a tree on the campground like some kind of ape himself—for eight months he sat, with little hills of lima beans (the Skunk Ape's favorite food) fanning out from his position in concentric circles on the ground. He waited, and waited, and eventually caught a short DV of what looks much like a man walking around in a gorilla suit, swinging his arms like an idiot. He got *The Daily Show* down to his place, likewise *Unsolved Mysteries*. He appealed to Collier County for a $40,000 tourism tax grant to help make widely known the creature living in the swamp on his property. Three and some years later the man is just as destitute as he was prior to the hullabaloo.

My coconspirator and I hit the road after work, blasting up through snowland Michigan in a whiteout for an hour, entering the "whore's mouth to Canada," as my coconspirator calls the city of Detroit, a full three later—1 a.m., deep into Eastern time. We put off Canada for another day, shuttling through manhole steam in the deserted city. Outside a single standing building on a block in the Cass corridor, where another old friend and conspirator lived, single men stood on separate street corners whacking themselves off to what little traffic there was.

We were met by my friend sleepy-eyed at his door. "Welcome to hell," he said.

22 FEB | In the haze of the morning's sleepiness I pondered the business of names, thinking that we none of us are much deserving of them, that it makes more sense just to be the lady, the coconspirator, the friend, the columnist, the Frenchman, the single man, the skunk ape. In any given moment in these lonely, American lives there can never be much more than one of each, anyhow.

Toronto is built in splendor, after Detroit. Tidy blocks, filled to the brim with life. No sign of the Frenchman. We got drunk and drunker and our Canadian host, taking us back to the apartment where we would bed down, apparently took offense at my coconspirator's admittedly bad joke about the reality of our sordid lives. "We need to go destroy ourselves!" he intoned with much gusto, to my ultimate amusement. "Well shit, we're already half there."

Truth, spoken with candor: not, unfortunately, something our Canadian host was prepared for. On the way up the stairs, he turned to my coconspirator and told him, "I don't like you. You can stay here cause you're his friend, but keep your distance from me, OK? I like him. But I do not like you."

"There's your Skunk Ape," my coconspirator repeated to me, later, amid giggles. "Drunk and disorderly."

I had to agree, though our Canadian host is a nice man, normally.

And my American coconspirator is, I'll admit, a bit of an ass.

23 FEB | Alain Robert, the Frenchman, is hidden, cloaked in Canadian secrecy. I should, rather could, be in the Southlands for all the smiles and shifty-eyed agreement I've gotten on the streets here. Like my Southern father and mother and aunts and uncles and Waffle House waitstaff over all the United States, these people talk like there's a fire behind their eyes. They'll say the object's over there, finger-pointing a three-flat, but it'll be dog shit right under your foot and you'll have to back up to where you started to get anyplace.

Damn the Frenchman! The CN Tower is nothing but a miniature Space Needle, even if it was built before the latter. Let's see the skunky little man climb that—further evidence of our ascendancy to the Canadians. God Bless US.

My coconspirator this evening is lost, off with a woman in an undisclosed section of town. Our Canadian host smiles tonight like nothing you've ever seen, he is so happy. And I am as well, for the moment. We sit with his wife around a television and have beers and watch *Strange Brew*, eat Korean food, seaweed and rice.

24 FEB | The trip is not a total bust.

"Got some change, brother?"

"Nah, but I got a cigarette, if you like."

"Hold up a second! Hold up just one second!" said the man, a large pack on his back, dreadlocks bouncing with his motion, backing off a little, a bright smile on his face and his hands open and flung up into the air over his head. "I know what's going on here! Germany, right?"

"Germany?" I said.

He pointed to my chest. "You're from Germany."

"Nah, I'm from South Carolina." Despite my Chicago residence, I would never get out of the mental grip of my hometown.

His smile widened even further. "Well goddamn, me too! I'm outta Camden. Where you from?"

"Rock Hill," I said.

"Whoa now! Spare a brother some change, will you?…"

We had nothing to spare, really, but told him that if he'd like to show us a bar in which we could watch the U.S. and Canada thrash each other for the Olympic gold in hockey without getting our asses kicked by drunk Canadians, we'd treat him to a beer or two, maybe some dinner.

"Aw shit," he said. He knew just the place.

At a spot just off the main that happened to be full to the tee of Americans, black men and a few women, mostly Southern transplants who pulled hard against the Americans—"You sure we're safe," I asked him, glancing around at all the Canada paraphernalia—the three of us got roaring drunk as the hockey match reached its apex. The crowd wildly cheered the white boys on skates adorned with maple leaves. Our table meekly applauded the boys in red, white and blue as they got whipped solidly in the last period.

We talked into the night as the streets outside filled full of honking cars with big flags lifted from their windows, men and women hollering the national pride. "Be careful, boys," our new friend said. "Be careful. There an umbrella out there," his hands reaching into the air above his head to describe an arc outward and down from both sides. "It covers everything. They know you're here. You got a cell phone?" He pointed to me. I told him I didn't. "It's a damn good thing," he said. "They keep you under it that way. But that's only one. A man can't get a thing done without them knowing. The longer you stay here the tighter you're under it."

"You mean in this bar?" I said. My coconspirator had begun to laugh and I punched him hard in the shoulder, shot him a look.

"This bar, this city, this country, man," the guy said. "Same shit, end of day."

My coconspirator laughed on.

"What's your name?" I said.

The man was positively shuddering now. He nudged his chair back from the table. "I'll keep that to myself," he said. My coconspirator laughed now louder, but the man did not get up.

"The least you could do," I muttered. Then I got mad at

both him and my asinine friend, who still hadn't stopped laughing.

"There's your Skunk Ape," my coconspirator managed to squeeze in, then bursting into a fit so wild I couldn't help but join in. Even the man across the table was tickled. "Who the hell you talking about, man? Not me, I hope. Skunk Ape! That old bullshit came up from Florida?" He chuckled a little more as my cohort bellowed on. "Hell, did you see the boy?" he said to me. "He was looking at me when he said it, but he was pointing at you." And the man shot his crooked finger my way. "Who's the Skunk Ape now?"

I could only nod soberly in agreement.

25 FEB | America, at last! I and my coconspirator got drunk in a bar upon our return. A lady I knew was there.

She was wearing a bear suit.

"Hello, lady," I said.

"I have a name," she said, drunkenly smiling.

"Meet my coconspirator," I said, showing her over to our corner table.

"Wow," he said to her. "What are you supposed to be? Alain Robert?"

She didn't get it, though my laughter was sufficiently contagious to prompt a chuckle, at least. Then she had to expect she was being made fun of when my coconspirator winked at me and I nearly fell over with the force of my laughter. After five more minutes of similar shenanigans, the lady left—rightly disgusted, I'd say.

We raised our glasses. "To the Skunk Ape," I said.

My subsequent convulsions sent five spent beer glasses crashing to their demise over the next hour.

Then we got kicked out.

 confederate yankee in the court of public opinion.

1) My term at the suburban religious college went off with little fanfare. I didn't much dig the theology they tried to teach me, much less believe in the god described in the books and the precious few tracts I might have put my head around, but I never let on. Most of the kids there could see the truth plain, so my circle was limited. A kid named Charlie, deeply devout, had been my only friend for a time, and he would eventually saunter off to state college in De Kalb and drink himself into twenty-something oblivion. I devised my own entertainment.

Out back of my folks' house, where I lived, I resurrected an old boyhood dumb show and altered it to suit. "Shoot the Horse From Under the Hanged Horse Thief" was its moniker, proceeding just as it sounded. I owned a noose long ago purloined from a novelty shop. I'd tie it around the netless rim above the dirt basketball court, into which I'd shot nothing since I was 10. The horse thieves were less imaginary friends than veritable hallucinations, my father and mother continuing on with their screaming inside the house and summoning in me the most rascally and disgusting characters. Here was Fob James, named after the Alabama governor, a reckless buffoon sentenced to death for the holdup of a convenience store.

I loaded the cap pistol—I'd had it even longer than the noose. POW POW POW! Firing in the air repeatedly, James' horse rearing up and then springing forward, leaving the two-bit criminal hanging, swinging from the noose, which I'd nudge with the tip of the cap pistol in assist if happen the wind wasn't blowing.

In the conjuring that followed, complete with trumpet fanfare and visions of myself as the Ugly, yes, of spaghetti-Western fame so ecstatic, I'd come to on my back on the dirt court, giant peals of laughter exploding from my chest.

I didn't know loneliness. I guess I wasn't necessarily too stupid to recognize the condition in the majority of my classmates, but I never let on. They didn't teach loneliness at the religious college, it was more an inherited trait of the pious young multi-sibling'd scholars there. They made straight *A*s. I made straight *B*s. They could have their loneliness.

My very last year at the school, when in November I'd turned a glorious 21 years of age, I became a semi-regular at a bar called the Cat's Alley on the road into my town, playing lazy man's poker in a dark, cloudy corner with a whitehaired man who was the most obvious, infamous cheat you'd ever witness. Somehow he and his cronies—a cabal typically of four younger men who sat as ducks to the man's game—managed to pull in dollar after dollar from whatever poor drunk soul decided he'd sit in on a hand or two. I never fully joined the party, never had all that much cash on hand to lose anything more than a beer purchase or two. But when I did play, if ever I lost as much as five bucks, I'd drunkenly swerve my father's 1976 Stingray the short way home. I aimed my cap pistol at shadow cops, criminals, imaginary liquor store clerks in a holdup along the way, popping shots out the window.

The May day before the zealots were to give me my B.S. in Criminology—"B.S., how fitting," Booker T. might have said—my mother called me in from the dirt. Father stood just by the front door, sunlight slanting in through the west-facing door's upper windows and lighting his hair up in a kind of halo, his eyes not rising from the floor when I entered with my mom on the crook of my arm. "Son," Father said, indicating the armchair across the small room. I sat down in it. My mother stood by my side. "You've heard us arguing," he said, "for many, many years." He scowled, pursed his lips, gestured toward me with outstretched arm. "This will come as no grand surprise."

I rolled my head around in the chair—I had a crick in my neck, born of craning upward to retie the noose outside not ten minutes prior.

"We've had enough of each other," he said. I took my contacts out and put them back in, took them out and put them back in, as he went on. The fuzzy orange glow of sun around my father's head took on a new life each time, growing in intensity as it lost focus.

My parents, Father told, were getting divorced.

Father Mr. Gregory Dilbert produced a slip of wrinkly white paper and indicated it was the title to the '76 Stingray, the car

almost as old as me. He was signing said title over. I would be
well provided for, he said. I liked that I couldn't really see him,
now. My contacts were long since secured in their white recep-
tacles. My father's shape thus I could tell moved my way, and I
found in my hand the title and what felt like a business card. I
took a minute in the intervening, queer silence to replace my
contacts. Indeed—GREGORY DILBERT, CLAIMS ADJUSTER,
MIDWEST CASUALTY. It had a St. Louis address and phone.

"Take good care of it," he said.

I couldn't help but imagine that he meant the card. "All right,
Pops," I said. "I'll be in touch." What was the value of my life?

My mother, incensed, distraught over the apparent numbness
of the exchange, burst into a fit of screaming and ran to her
bedroom.

THEY failed to immediately mention that they wanted me
out of the house. When finally they did, two days later, I drove
at my father's direction to a relatively new but cheaply built and
thus prematurely dilapidated apartment complex by I-55 I
would spend the summer in at their expense until I could find a
job someplace, they were oh so hopeful, in the city. I stared at a
map all night, hoping I suppose to deduce opportunity in the
city's design, but I knew only where the men in suits roamed,
where the tall buildings were. Practicality, a decision made on a
plan of action, was not in the cards this night.

Around midnight I went to the Cat's Alley.

After three beers alone, I was out of cash. Still, I approached
the men at the roundtable in back, hoping for a couple games,
gratis. "We know you," said the old man, motioning for me to
sit down. "What do you have?"

I laid my tattered cash-poor wallet on the table's rough-hewn
surface, removing my driver's license.

The old man stared at the wallet for close to a full minute,
exchanging the occasional inscrutable glance with the men
around the table, with me. "It won't do," he said. He idly began
to shuffle. He dealt, always—'twas how he won with such con-
sistency, I knew.

I ran outside and dug from the Stingray's little backseat my
noose, cap pistol, and a cowboy shirt adorned with stitched
images of galloping horses just over the breast pockets, one I'd
not worn since I was 12. I kept it for those ugly sentimental
reasons people keep all sorts of things, I guess—things without

utility: notes from high-school sweethearts, valentines from third grade, pens used to draw maps of undiscovered planets. New horizons inserted themselves into my field of vision. In retrospect, it makes perfect that I would fail.

But you can convince yourself of anything in the heat of whatever moment. In this late-blooming summer, I sucked in the cool air, puffed up my chest and then strode through the bar's vestibule, through its old-timey swinging doors, stomping deliberately to the roundtable. I laid the pistol, shirt, noose on the table, where they joined my empty wallet in shabby splendor. The old man thought it was some kind of joke. "What do we want with this stuff?" he said, eyes narrowed under the white cloud of his hair.

"Me and you," I said.

I would punish the old man, punish him for his swindling. I believed it.

The men around the table laughed. The old man laughed. "Is that a damn noose?" he said.

"To string you up with," I said, dramatically dragging a stool across the floor from the bar to a spot across from the old man, who laughed. He planted a $50 bill on his side of the table and dealt five card draw in apparent deference to youth and inexperience in spite of my cockiness. My hand: best case scenario it might wield two pair. I discarded three, retrieved three, and ended not with two pair but a single, a two of clubs and a two of diamonds. I slammed it down confidently, though, the cap pistol bouncing a clatter out upon the table as the old man spread in a quick flourish a straight flush, full 10 to ace, all of hearts, and the table exploded in laughter.

Defining moments in one's life come unexpectedly. If I hadn't asked for this, I'd done little to prevent it. I drove home in silence, without even the Stingray's AM radio to accompany me. Halfway there, I realized I'd left my driver's license sitting atop the roundtable with the rest of the detritus. I cried, a little, back at my apartment. But I vowed there in that near silence that someday, somehow, I'd get it all back.

MY mother was on the train as soon as I was out the door, I found out. She called me the next day from Vicksburg, where she was holed up in her sister's home just outside town with a tub of ice cream and a remote control. "Springer's on," she said, then went off on a tirade about how I needed to go out and get a job, how the money they gave me wouldn't last, my father was a bum, a bum! she said. Did I know that the bastard had life-insurance policies on the both us? She didn't know how the hell he did it, but he himself was the beneficiary! She couldn't afford, she said, bailing me out of every goddamn bad thing that happened.

I cried a little, but the more I thought on the general chaos I grew less weary, channeling the associated energy. I motored to the nearest service station and picked up a copy of the Sunday paper, in which I spotted an advertisement requesting a clown, one that would cull real belly-laughs at Heights Rodeo just south of the city. Dress the part. Apply in person.

Two days later, a Tuesday, I put on a leather vest—another leftover, this from a childhood pageant—I could hardly get around my chest even with nothing underneath but a frail white undershirt. At the Joliet Salvation Army I found a pair of slacks with a 48-inch waist, red with silver pin-striping, in which I stuck a pillow over my backside, then bouncing my way down the freeway and back toward the city to the rodeo.

The parking lot sat above the ring itself on an odd low hill in the otherwise flat landscape. A show was on. Anxiety sent its little needles through me, an electric jolt to my stomach, which fell down below the loose belt on my pants. I remained buckled in the seat and watched, over the Stingray's high front wheel wells, the rowdy crowd of black men and women who filled the bleacher rows on each side of the ring, a big oval, more or less, paved only with dirt, woodchips in spots. The spectators loomed loud and respectable, families dressed as if for church and chanting wildly for the riders, who rode so furiously they ripped from mules bounds as high as those of any comparable horse.

I had my father's old watch-chain hung from my belt, a can of Kiwi black shoe polish in place of the broken watch once there. I took ten minutes blacking my face, then jammed the can into the inner pocket of the vest, rising gingerly from the Corvette, waddling down along the walk in front of the bleachers. Men and women in the front rows screamed and laughed at me, alternately, variously, the proceedings generally no more than a wall of red-faced shame. A half-eaten hot dog came screaming by my left ear, missing by inches.

A leader will smile like that when asking for your soul, I thought, gaze intent then on the wide smile of the extremely tall man in top hat making his way up the walk. "Identification, please," said Booker T. Washington, as he'd introduced himself. He smiled like he knew the joke and there was absolutely no way you could possibly understand what he meant. "Identification," he repeated. Like the damn shoe polish all over your face wasn't enough humiliation.

"I got nothing," I said, reaching into my empty front pants pockets as if in confirmation. I threw my arms out, palms up.

Booker T. laughed.

Then I remembered the business card in my back pocket. "My father," I said. "Casualty claims, as it says." I tried a smile at the man, now, tried very hard to feel it, but he only parroted it back at me, his wide eyes and now pursed lips barely turned up at the corners imparting the happy scorn I might have expected, I guess.

I almost lost my nerve, I did, but Booker T. said, "So you want to be a clown, obviously. Not bad so far, but the blackface is unnecessary here."

I sucked in a deep breath, setting my arms akimbo and jutting out my chest, one of the vest's buttons popping off and flying up over Booker T.'s top hat. I ripped the can of shoe polish from its chain and flung it into the audience. Booker was nodding approvingly now.

"I am Mambo!" I proclaimed. "King of clowns!" A new feeling ran through my veins and arteries—the certainty of a design shoddily built but valiantly pursued, the rush of possibility. I channeled high-school insults and all the horror of my recent days and flung them with my open right hand straight across Booker T.'s left cheek. An uproarious guffaw blew down from the bleachers. I grinned up into the crowd, then back to Booker, who frowned, adjusting his necktie. He cleared his throat. "Now that's more like it," he said, tipping his hat and wagging his head, smiling. He strode forward, picked me up and threw me over the railing into the rodeo ring, wild with the time.

2) For a week I came at the job with as much brazen pathos as the riders did. You'd figure mules would shamble like old mutts, cross-breeds as they are, good for nothing but packing up and moving along—or being packed up, diddled by farm retards—but the riders pushed them and the few horses there to the limit and got tossed willy-nilly about the rodeo ring. The cowboys customized the beasts to their needs, riding without sad-

dles, horsewhip-leather reins tied in knots around the brutes' necks like to choke them into submission—but having the opposite effect. The men's spurs worked well, too, and I got many a laugh getting kicked around by the beasts, nostrils flared and eyes rolling as they booted me in my padded ass. I discovered a talent for tumbling, flying through the air and down into various permutations of rolls, back up as the beasts charged. I'd jump, bound up and over like a championship bullfighter, hands on the mule's ears, its momentum propelling my legs high above me and over. It amazed me, the velocity, the energy.

And the surprising benevolence, if it didn't extend to wages. I got paid 25 cents an hour for my acrobatics, but I also got to play the slave in Booker T.'s plantation game. The man began inviting me over for dinner nearly immediately after Mambo's initial appearance at Heights Rodeo, and Booker T. even kept up his own part in the charade, calling me by my adopted name even while his wife, done up in an old mammy costume and reminding me first of the Aunt Jemima of pancake syrup fame, second of some half-forgotten old-movie character with a silly scarf over her head and whose breasts were large enough to make her back ache constantly, doled out long-simmered turnip greens, cornbread, fried chicken, black-eyed peas to fuel my slow roll toward contentment.

And then there was the matter of Booker's daughter, a six-foot-tall big-breasted jewel of a 13-year-old forever in a thin white undershirt too small for her frame. Lalena. Booker seemed to relish putting me through the temptation of her slow saunter into the dining room, night after night, the exaggerated process by which she took her seat, long bend of her upper body out over the table, doe eyes and fluttering lashes aimed up above my head. I was not the first to endure slave status, I found, as Lalena had gained the first signs of her outrageous womanhood at age 11. "Many have come before," Booker toasted me one fine summer evening, "but none daresay had the skills of the young Mambo. To the clowns!" And we drank.

It was criminal, surely, but I felt the need to indulge James Washington, Booker T., in his peculiar fantasy. And if not the need, surely the want. The food was good, and there were moments of sublimity, when from just under the playacting emerged a reality not unwholesome, not unlike my imaginary kinship with men of the law in the distant, wild Western lands of mere weeks prior.

I even propositioned Booker to join me out at the Cat's Alley one night, expecting an opportunity for retribution, deliverance from the devil that haunted my imagination in the form of the white-haired old cardsharp. Booker accepted, to my utter surprise, but the old man and his cronies were nowhere to be found. The bartender, a former steel worker—redneck, more or less—remembered me, though, and when I told Booker my story the bartender overheard and turned to me, shaking his head with shame for ever being associated with the patrons of the Cat's Alley. He would later quit, I guess. I never saw him again.

"The guilt of the white people is astounding," Booker T. said, this night, as the bartender sulked around the back bar.

"It's shame, my friend, not guilt," I said.

"You're right," he said.

"But don't you go assigning those qualities to me."

"Of course not, Mambo," he said. "You are beyond shame." He turned back his whiskey, then ordered another round—I was scarcely halfway through mine. "I have a feeling you will get what you want," he went on. "Just remember that sometimes that means backing up and deciding what that is itself. You might be amazed by how it's sometimes right there in front of you."

I nodded at this armchair wisdom with little conviction but was happy for the moment. Whiskey was in front of me: I did not pay for it. I drank and Booker T. and I moved on to lighter topics of conversation. Mule breeding requires a stable of horses and donkeys. The Heights crowd were experimentalists well-known in the field.

THE ride from Joliet to Heights was killing me on expenses, just as my mother foretold, and one momentous evening in the ring my right hand slipped down a mule's neck during a vertical bound, index finger lodging securely underneath the tight swath of leather around the brute's neck. The monstrous creature jerked with my weight atop him, snapping my finger. Of course, the lack of employer-provided insurance on a 25-cent wage was a foregone conclusion, and, asked about a raise, Booker just looked sternly down his flat nose, a difficult prospect in and of itself, and murmured a bit about tradition, my friend, tradition.

No clowns' union anywhere outside the borders of such far-flung locales as Texas, if there, I left Heights with only slightly heavy heart a few nights later, my mangled finger healing fast a near 45 degrees off-kilter. I wheeled the Stingray toward Joliet with my left hand, biting my bottom lip against the pain with every shift. I thought of calling my father in St. Louis but felt sure he'd just chastise me for spending my inheritance on college only to join a rodeo, a black one at that, the racist. I called my mother, predictably, in that decrepit Mississippi town and listened to her talk of how white and fat she had gotten over the two months she'd been there, spread over her recliner days on end. She hadn't left the house in weeks but for the paper, cigarettes. Though there was this nice policeman named Norb who came by now and again and...

"Jesus, Mother! Jesus, please," I spat into the receiver, then spent the next three days between crying jags trying not to imagine my mother and the policeman doing surely nasty, forbidden things. A gathering storm, an expulsion of the nastiness of my heritage, perhaps, for at the end of the time—three weeks, give or take—I resolved that a reentry into the world of masters of their own destinies was appropriate.

The humiliation of Heights felt hyperreal, after all, cartoonish in intensity.

Booker was sad to see me quit, even after only little more than a month. He'd had grand visions of white/black harmony coming through the union of young Dewey Dilbert, he said, eyes wide, and the budding Lalena, but he wouldn't up the pay. "Tradition 30 years running," he said. None of the clowns lasted very long, of course, which was something of a problem: most of the folks who attended the rides at the ring came in large part to see the clowns kicked around, he said. "When we lose one, it's a big blow to business."

The man at least agreed to pay for the proper treatment of my finger. It was healing into a shape more suitable to a boomerang as we spoke.

If I ever needed anything else, Booker told me, come on back. He might have other work for me. I figured he was just blowing smoke, being nice.

I was beginning to know lonelinesss. I bought a new wallet, a pair of horn-rimmed spectacles to replace my dull contact lenses, and drove the Stingray into an inner-city neighborhood that held the questionable attribute of being known as "up-and-coming." The first night I was there somebody stole the wallet right from my back pocket, which I interpreted in my woe as an act of divine intervention, thus keeping back my tears.

But I rented an apartment and lucked my way into a job downtown as a "Surveillance Analyst" soon enough. I sat hour by hour by day watching videos of the comings and goings of various state departments' employees in the Albert Parsons Center. Angelica, a svelte customer service rep for the division of waste management, smoked illicit cigarettes in the back stairwell on break while talking of the things Jesse did to her last night. While she smoked and talked, the audience, a lady from the other side of the building, twirled the beauty's own hair into braids like a schoolgirl on the playground. Angelica didn't seem to mind. Two weeks into the routine, which I clinically observed, the two were blocking the doors to the stairwell and smoking pot. Another two weeks and they were straddling each other with black-rubber dildos strapped into place and thrust into the appropriate openings. I damn near swooned right there in my cubicle.

But, recovering, I looked on with outrage, heat, a painful hard-on that made me sick to my stomach. Thereafter, I avoided the channel to that particular camera, though in weak moments the impulse arose at just the wrong, or right, time.

Billy Jones was a different story. The finger-wagging Southerner began his campaign to unseat me a couple days after the news of Angelica had reached the greater offices' populations. He approached me with a quick intro and handshake. The ruffian could've used a uniform upgrade, though I suspect his disregard for the office dress code was willful—he wore a white T-shirt stained faintly yellow at the pits, black corduroy pants that looked so frayed they could turn to dust with little more than a sneeze on his part. If Booker T. was a model of benevolence with slightly twisted intentions, Jones was pure effrontery, known for smoking in the office just to see how much he could get away with. "I want to see that shit," Billy said one day well along in his campaign. His head bobbed in a nod, the big mop of unruly curly hair up there bouncing with it.

"Do you work here?" I said. I was learning a bit from him, after all.

He shot a sideways glance my way and, smiling, promptly tore the nameplate—DEWEY DILBERT, PARSONS CENTER SURVEILLANCE—from the outer wall of my cubicle and strode off.

I launched my own campaign. It partly stemmed from a desire for revenge, partly from a healthy awareness of the value of entertainment, things to get one through the day-to-day. Billy's shaggy-headed defiance of the hygiene code I recorded in detail in a three-ring binder-cum-log book devoted to the finger-wagging Southerner, clipping a Confederate flag image from a biker magazine I picked up at a kiosk in the Parsons Center's public area and gluing it to the front of the binder, designated B - I - L - L - Y in large capitals. He stopped by my desk often. Apart from stealing my desk's nameplate, the man's specialty was in loudly proclaiming to me how much he wanted my job, what with the free pornography and all. But after a time I could see he came by simply out of a high-toned narcissism—he wanted to see himself on the big screen, a 10-inch monitor that sat on the aluminum shelf that was my desk.

He knew too well of my surveillance, of course, which in any case I wasn't attempting to hide from him. "Let me see that nasty one," he said a particularly lackluster yet stunningly momentous Friday, referencing a camera seduction that was his "greatest hit," he said, as I fast-forwarded through it toward other matters. I could tell he was hungover. His typical white T-shirt/black-corduroy uniform was unusually rumpled, even for him.

"The play is rather convincing," I said. I swiveled around to face the man, Billy standing as usual with an elbow propped on my cubicle's wall, my nameplate in his hand, just barely inside. He lit a cigarette today in the nonsmoking office and nodded. I crossed my legs and leaned my own elbow back on the desk. "Hell," I said, "if I was a chick I'd go for it." I don't know if I meant it. Billy had a rather modern dandy-type hipster sensibility that undoubtedly endeared his shaggy-headed self to women of rakish good looks, old fags too.

"Really?" Billy said, seemed genuinely in shock, wagging his head a bit and closing his eyes as if to imagine his image in my mind. He puffed on his cigarette.

Then the phone rang.

I may not have picked it up if it weren't for the sense that it might get Billy on to whatever he was supposed to be doing, even if I was indeed enjoying the pathetic excuse for banter we had going.

I rather wish I hadn't.

My phone seldom rang.

It was the Mississippi State Police, as I told Billy promptly after I hung up—he seemed to have sensed something amiss in my quiet groans into the receiver, stuck around smoking his cigarette perhaps half-suspecting a revelation of sorts to spring forth. I had one for him. "My mother has been killed," I said.

He froze, his face pinched and twisted. "A man in a cape just jumped," he said.

I didn't know what he was talking about.

"Your mother's in Mississippi?" he said. "I'll be hanged by my danged ears. Christ, man, what's she doing there?" I had nothing for him. He gestured with my nameplate, said thanks, stuffing it in the back pocket of his corduroys, flung his head back to get the curls away from his eyes and stubbed the cigarette out in a smoldering hole in the carpet, all in the same motion. He strode off.

I would learn much in the hours that followed, chief among the details that the reality of the building's design prompted hosts of suicides, more than any other in the city. Visitors typically jumped from the 23rd-floor viewing area to their deaths in the atrium of the fancy hotel-like administrative building. Billy'd seen a caped man in the act. Billy'd just had an altercation with the boss. Billy had just called the man a "dwarf turd" and quit in a rage moments before our unusually protracted encounter. When I learned all of this, I was close to walking right out on the man's heels. I figured I'd never survive another day in the cubicle without the boy's antics to keep me entertained, at once ahead of the investigative curve.

So, two days later, after learning next to none of the specifics surrounding my mother's death—but for the fact that she was killed dead by a deep-tanned Vicksburg cop gone crazy over being burned stone blind by her body, which he wanted all his own—I quit.

I would never see my mother again—the pain of this fact was curiously muted. I had nothing to do with the settling of affairs. My father apparently became a regular on the Mississippi trail down to Vicksburg. In the months ahead her death receded quickly like all memories, the shrillness of her voice on the phone, her unreserved capacity for melodrama, her clear love for her son. All of this, blown away.

3)I took to the windswept battery that was my up-and-coming neighborhood's streets. The following Monday. It had been a long, bitter winter in the downtown office. I inquired with the record shop first, where I figured my horn-rimmed spectacles might endear me to the music-nerd crowd behind the counter. I asked one of the geeks whether a position was open. The boy replied in a false British accent, saying, "Position for you? I'm afraid not, sir," before going immediately back to whatever cataloging he was doing in the old vinyl shelves behind the counter. I rode the force of the slap back outside among the roaring motorbikes of spring, the women in short skirts with carefully sculpted hairdos ablaze in the new-summer sunlight. *Woe unto me!* I quite exactly thought. *I can't even make an impression on vapid shop clerks! Which is to say nothing of my truly pathetic nature!*

I did not shed a tear, though. I turned into the hip café on the block and applied as a waiter, was promptly denied, refused, thrown out again on my tired legs into the street.

The sun was bright, warm, the women and girls sleeveless, the rolls of flesh in their armpits visible and reminding me briefly of my mother and her killer. Her ashes, my aunt told, had been scattered over a reservoir outside Vicksburg from the end of a famous pier with an infamous name. The trial was not over. I'd received word that my father sued the ruined town for her wrongful death, which I wasn't sure was legit, and was assured of impending victory. The bastard proclaimed a $20,000 value on her life, though a third party went higher.

I pressed my forehead into the hip café's large front display windows and closed my eyes, then pressing my nose into the glass. I felt something pass out of my chest in a gentle sucking there, body fully forgoing another attempt at a job search in favor something lighter, better, perhaps an ice cream cone, a beer. I opened my eyes and looked straight into the face and blatantly direct stare of one of the record shop clerks, who was poised mannequin-like over a latte at the café's window table. The clerk spooned his drink, shook his head like a disapproving old maid.

I moved over and pressed my nose into the porous brick of the building's façade, the force of a high anger fixing my flesh into the pores so that it clung for a moment when I moved away, wincing at the pull and pop. Billy stood up the sidewalk a bit in his customary white T-shirt and corduroy but with a white bandage around the whole of his head. He was in front of the lately arrived corporate coffeeshop—the neighborhood's denizens no doubt having pled for their savior and said savior bubbling and farting steamed milk and hissing steam through fresh-ground espresso to palpitate the hearts and exhaust the arteries of the would-be rich and destitute alike, without discrimination.

"Dewey," Billy said. He shook his bandaged head like a rocker, raising his 100-percent post-consumer-waste-made cup.

"What's up, man?"

"Looking for work," I said, tipping my horn rims to the man.

"I just applied here," he said, pointing through the glass and up into the faux rafters girding the upper interior of the corporate coffeshop. "They're hiring, at least."

I grinned—mentally, only. "What happened to your head? Looks painful."

"Long story," he said. "Let's just say a bottle was shattered over it." And now he smiled, too, tipping me good-bye for the second time this week with two fingers to his forehead as he walked away. I had to follow.

I passed full into the infamous corporate coffeeshop and applied, got the job a few weeks later, was granted the position of Assistant Manager, and had to be at least a little grateful for my own personal savior, now, though said savior quickly threatened to go out of business.

Another franchise had opened right across the street just lateral to the train station and commanded more effectively the divided attentions of the neighborhood, the bearded proprietors at the hip café down the street, the strangely nerdy record-shop clerks, the denizens young and old and rich and poor whose collective eyes teared up at the happiness of the better choice, leaving little room for my own shop. Impending economic doom nationwide didn't help, either, in the midst of the post-9/11 stock-market turmoil as we were. (The neighborhood, I thought, felt primed to return to its former non-up-and-coming status, yuppies fleeing, crime rate plummeting, properties drying up.) The savior left me jobless yet again, closing its doors a mere three years into my highly caffeinated expedition there. Though it didn't matter that much. I'd saved a little money, after all.

Besides, it did little else for me, absolutely nothing with the art-school girls I met at the up-and-coming neighborhood's bars, who sent me bucking my mule back at home on the toilet the minute they found out where I worked.

And yes, as the coffeeshop threw its patrons and employees both to the better alternative, their stabilizing neighborhoods, their newly-renovated and increasingly unprofitable real estate, I was struck with the memory of the origins of my careering, venturing then far south a lonely Friday morning and Booker T. greeting me with closed fists, his shoulders darkening the doorway to his bungalow. I hung back on the street while the man stood tall, menacing atop his porch steps. I removed my glasses, got down on my knees, and pled with the Master of Ceremonies for recognition. "I have come back," I said. "You told me to!" I reached for my wallet and ID and, finding nothing, was struck with yet another, more powerful recollection even as the man strode down the steps and grasped the collar of my shirt, pulling me to my feet.

"I do know you," he said, but he did not smile. I could feel the heat of the man's breath on my face.

He dropped me in a pile on the street. A gaggle of neighborhood boys crowded round me, their faces inscrutable, and minutes later I found Booker T. wading through them to lift me from the ground and carry me inside, a grin of recognition long since spread over his face.

Over turnip greens, I asked after the status of the rodeo these past years. Fine, just fine, Booker said, though they'd been going with a black clown of late, and paying him well. Times had been hard since the shakedown the "Lay It Up," he said, had engineered.

"The lay it what?"

"Lay it up," Booker said. "The Local Association for the Advancement of Uncolored People."

"You can't be serious."

"Quite serious," he said.

I thought. "Where's the 'it' come in?"

"Half shit," he said, "I suppose."

LALENA had been married in my absence to one of the riders. Gerald Watchmaker broke records, Booker said. "He's the real deal." They'd shacked up in a small house near the ring where Lalena now held court as master of ceremonies at the tender age of 17. Booker, meanwhile, engaged other pursuits. The two of us located, two weeks later, a 1976 Stingray in a Gary junkyard almost identical to my old car, fiberglass body miraculously intact. Booker gave it a working over, and I commandeered it and an old Winchester rifle Booker T. gave me in honor of my return on less-than-aboveboard missions to headquarters of competing rodeos in the area and other enemies of the aging master of ceremonies, including a journey to the offices of the LAA'IT'UP with a tire iron for the structure's windows. I was happy for the action, really, and accordingly in due time I found myself back in Joliet snooping around my childhood home under cover of eerily dark suburban night.

There was an odd couple living in the dilapidated, counterfeit farmhouse, two gay men who drove big Lexus rides. I caught sight of them kissing through the rear kitchen windows, from my vantage behind the bushes in turn behind the old basketball goal in the yard. The next day, I bought a corduroy suit and posed as a real-estate agent, selling them on half the rent of my own apartment back in the city, convincing the couple of the admittedly false value of the neighborhood with the dexterity possible only of a deluded resident. I quietly paid the other half of the rent by way of a handshake deal brokered with my landlord, a German immigrant who seemed impressed with the shadiness of it all in spite of its relatively innocuous quality.

Life took on the surreality of a dream or that fizzling head game just before the dream became the reality. I gave up quick on any design toward actually working in real estate that may have crossed my mind, settled in with Booker T., the former master of ceremonies, whose fingers were now in all sorts of cash-rich pies. I would be no clown. I rode around wildly romantic with the Winchester propped in the Stingray's passenger seat. I was deep into Joliet, where I attempted to channel the thing so many lives are blessed with: manna of sweet forgetfulness.

4)But most memories aren't easy or necessarily desirable to ride oneself of. I picked up Booker T. for a round at the Cat's Alley one fine evening, the name of the place itself burned into my consciousness nostalgic-sweet and surreptitious. I packed the rifle behind the Stingray's seats; Booker wore two pistols, one in a concealed holster under his trenchcoat, the other tucked into his belt.

I strode into the bar proud but at once uneasy at the familiarity of the bartender's gray beard, his mustache, the longhaired mustachioed patrons and their mean white smirks that turned in unison upon the creak of the swinging doors. "Howdy," I said, adjusting my horn rims.

We laid our elbows on the old bar and had three beers and three whiskeys apiece without saying a word. Men played poker off in a dim corner across the stool-littered space. "I've lost something, hear?" I said finally. "Here." I laid a finger hard on the bar to bring the point home.

Booker nodded. One of the mustachioed pool men sat down on the other side of Booker. "Will keeps the lost and found behind the counter there," he said. The bartender's pointed beard jabbed his chest repeatedly with his own head-nodding.

"Ahh," I said, motioning for the old cardboard box, which I proceeded to rifle through, pocketing one of four rusty Zippo lighters therein. "I was thinking more like in a card game," I said, pushing the box back across the bar. I turned round and nodded to the men in the corner. Two hanging lights over the bar barely reached the men spread round their smoky table. "I lost something in card game," turning back to the bartender.

"Watch it," the mustachioed man said. "Those boys are carrying."

I shrugged, turning back to what would be my last whiskey tonight, to Booker. "Why Booker T. Washington?" I asked. "Why not Martin Luther or Richard Wright? Hell, even W.E.B.? Booker T.'s got a reputation for, well, you know…"

"Yeah," Booker T. said. "You might tell my mother Martha and father George the same. Wasn't like I had much choice in the matter." He rattled the ice around in his glass. Will the bartender supplied him with a fourth whiskey. "Beer too," Booker said.

The card players in the corner were feline-quiet, the white-haired man among them. I rose from my stool, confrontational determination to my movements, and quickly strode over, slowing and circling the table, thumbs stuck in my belt loops for effect. After two revolutions I prized a stool and squeezed into a space to the right of the old man. "Mind if I sit in on a few?" I said, much louder than was necessary.

The crowd did not respond.

I watched five players fold in quick succession to the outrageous $200 raise the white-haired man then laid down. Only another guy nearly as old as the white-haired one himself had the gall to see him, then promptly call the round. I pegged the guy for a newcomer, which he was. The old dealer cheat threw down a full house, three aces and two 10-cards. Two of the aces were of hearts.

"This old man's a fluke," I said. "A cheater. You boys know that, don't you?"

The table remained silent but for the newcomer, who took the moment to very deliberately point out the fact of the cheat's two aces of hearts. A few men then reached under the table, upper bodies moving along with their hands as if to sit up to hitch their jeans. "No need to pull the guns now," I said. "My man Booker T. Washington's got the drop on the lot of you anyhow." I nodded slowly to the bar and heads turned and there sat the big trench-coated man poised on his stool under a hanging light, pistols drawn and trained on the shadowy figures at the table. I stepped wide around the table and motioned Booker T. closer. "Now," I said, "I figure I'm owed something."

The men shot glances around the table at one another.

"You," I pointed to the old cheat. A groan issued forth from the men as he stood. "They're not so quick to upbraid you, are they?" I said. A younger sort with his back to Booker's pair of pistols went quick for his own. Booker T. plugged a shot from his right-hand pistol to the back of the man's neck before he even turned—he slumped, wheezing briefly, onto the table. "Well, maybe they are," I said, "but even so you'll all play hell getting around Booker T."

No one moved.

I addressed the old cheat. "Yes, I figured you owe me something. I figure the interest on what you stole from me in five years is equal now to at least double what it was. That'd be two empty wallets, two cap pistols, and two nooses, one of which I figure we could use to string you up like you deserve, cheating these boys for years."

The man simply nodded. I felt invincible, invulnerable, like nothing before.

"Can you produce them?" I said. "The originals, minus the interest, will be just fine. I'll get interest enough out of watching you sweat."

The movie played itself out in the old man's nods, with them the sweat sliding down his brow. We moved quickly to tie his hands and squeeze him into the rear of the Corvette. I laid the Winchester across my lap as we drove, quickly, to a warehouse in a west-side Chicago ghetto, the old man leading us. The exchange was made, and we packed him in again, drove down to 45th and State and gave him over to a crowd of boys. It was a Friday night, hot. We figured we'd made their day.

AFTERWARD, I strung the old noose from my boyhood's disused basketball hoop, fired high shots with the cap pistol days on end. I missed my mother and Angelica and Booker T., when the two of us weren't meeting to plan the next item of business. I got bored with "Shoot the Horse From Under the Hanged Horse Thief" rather quickly. I got fat, too, figuring all the while my mother's genes didn't help the matter.

Then Booker T. Washington was arrested. They tried him for the slaying of one Maynard Caldwell, of Romeoville. He would've been sentenced and probably promptly killed outright by a mob had it not been for my intervention. I was fed up with lying around, progressively inheriting my mother's legacy, protected divinely by Booker's silence regarding my identity in the courtroom.

I was after eternal life. Trust me, though, it's not what you're thinking.

The jury was out only time enough for you to smoke a cigarette, if you did that sort of thing. When they were about to issue the verdict, I oozed fat and flatulent through the front door with the Winchester raised high and trained on the judge, to the gasping awe of the middling crowd on hand, the mass either side of me shrinking back from my figure in small waves as I waddled forward, farting. "I wish to die for this man," I proclaimed. The judge quivered, the barrel of the Winchester no more than two feet from the old man's nose.

He attempted a shrug to the bailiff, which came off more like a seizure. I farted. The bailiff didn't know what the hell to do, so he dropped his gun belt and ran screaming from the courtroom. "OK, then," the judge said.

"My father didn't teach me shit," I said down the Winchester's long barrel, directly to the judge. "I am tired, and fat, and lazy, and I want to die. And if I ever did learn anything from the old man, it's that human life has a value." The judge shook his head like he didn't understand. "He's a claims adjuster," I said. "Casualty. And so that he don't get a thing for me, I wish to be hanged, to die honorably. I give myself up. And I want you to pronounce it, in exchange for Booker T. here's freedom. It'll go like so: we sentence Mr. Dewey Dilbert, of Joliet, Illinois, me, to be hanged by the neck till he be dead, dead—" The hall filled with the sound of cannon fire. I felt the carpeted floor against my cheek. I looked up, as high as I could, to find the terrified bailiff standing over me with his foot on the rifle, which lay next to me. Booker T. I saw slumped over his defendant's table— they'd shot him, too.

And some of what they say is true. Body consciousness is the last to go. In a dream I followed Booker through a door of his choosing and into a small blackness utterly complete, the blackness of an isolation cell. Which blackness was imbued with heat so extreme I cried out soundlessly for what seemed like an eternity. But out of the blackness, out of the heat, after that eternity, came motion and light, freedom.

BOOKER lived the rest of his life in prison. I was scattered in a high lake wind over the rodeo ring at Heights, where my remains endure to imbue the place with the carnivalesque sense it needs. I speak through Lalena, to a certain extent. I am one with the winds, the dust kicked up off the shoes of the mules. But I am also the consciousness of the crowd, the joy and the pain, the hilarity.

"White Mambo" lighters and watch chains are big sellers at the gift stalls during gala weekend shows.

My father sued the city of Joliet, predictably, for my wrongful death and was compensated half the full $300,000 value he himself might have adjusted. He quit his job, bought a home near the water in Biloxi on the Mississippi Gulf Coast. He was a regular at the blackjack tables, where he became known as the Confederate Yank, scourge of the Southlands. He was good, he won.

ZOO.

HIGH winter and Essie Mae Washington-Williams was on TV promoting her memoir, *Dear Senator*, about her semi-clandestine life as the illegitimate African-American daughter of the United States' most notorious former segregationist. A picture of myself and said segregationist—he must've been in his 70s at the time, I was perhaps three—sits atop the mantle above the fake fireplace in my Chicago apartment. The old man looks happy enough, I guess, seemingly without a thought in his mind about any possible justification for his past, an interpretation I would make again and again, in my teenage years, meeting him repeatedly at various functions and being presented with the unfortunate opportunity to shake his limp, liver-spotted hand.

In the picture, the only one that I have from my prepubescent Carolina life, I am engaged in an activity whose legacy would follow me far into adulthood, a nervous fidgeting of hands. Strom Thurmond holds my three-year-old body high, and I'm doing my best, goddamnit, just to avert my eyes, I think, my baby hands poised in front of me, fingers half interlocked, nothing to hold on to but the old man's face but God help us if I reached out for that.

I leave the picture on the mantle to remind me of the bigoted enemy out there.

Visitors to my apartment get a kick out of it, too.

Essie Mae wasn't the only news item that season—it was a winter of repeat presidential inauguration for the done-up-and-come son of a Connecticut Yankee turned Texas cowpoke, a season of hurrah and hooray and guttural and disgusting huzzahing to the man's evermore false message—America an economic ivory tower underpinned by a veritable caveman outlook, beset upon by the moral equivalent of club-wielding barbarians and responding in kind. Apropos, I wanted to do something dirty. I wanted to throw eggs at limousines on inauguration day as many of my upstanding Neanderthal friends were planning. That was the answer, I'd determined upon returning to Chicago from my folks' home after Christmas, eggs that would crack and whose insides would dry on the black paint job, and woe to he or she who attempted to remove the dried remnants—a heinous fated awaited. Some kids hit my own American sedan once, and two weeks later, when finally the Chicago snow that had buried the bottom half of the vehicle sufficiently melted to grant access to the car's driver-side door, I realized the calamity, proceeding to scour the spot with the heinously smelly sponge with which I commonly washed my dishes at the time. A mere five minutes in I'd ruined the paint job—the frozen egg remnants came off with application of hot water, but so did the color—further even than the numerous long key scratches on its flank already had, which is to say, irreparably.

Today I smoke. A lot. I like having something in my hands. If they're empty and I find myself in a situation where things are expected of me—say I'm on the job, editors are asking questions about something I was supposed to do (maybe I did, maybe I didn't)—my first instinct is to roll and light a cigarette and blow the smoke into the interlocutor's face. Essie Mae Washington-Williams' much more deferential personality manifested itself on the radio program, and I'd assume in the book though I'll most certainly never read it, in a reflex action to continually apologize for the segregationist senator. Again, I wouldn't have been so charitable. I walked out to work that day fuming a little, laughing all the while, at the preposterous history of the recently dead century-old man, to happen upon every window in my car shattered and a note scrawled on the back of a Spanish leaflet for a local grocery, whose edges fluttered in the slight winter breeze and which read, "motherfucker my chair bitch I know u."

Chickens coming home to roost. Bad karma. I'd been on something of a crusade since the last snowstorm. In the time-honored American tradition of the citizenry's utter lack of participation in anything resembling a community or society, my neighborhood's denizens were using old lawn chairs and bits of board and other urban detritus to reserve "their" parking spaces in the public way while their cars were parked elsewhere—at work, for instance, or the grocery. To be fair, some street spaces were absolutely immaculate, having been shoveled dry by said denizens, while others, like the one where I'd been parked, were still buried a foot deep in snow but for tire tracks angling in and out of the street's center right of way. But I had indeed shoveled, if only a little, and after digging at four or five different spots over the course of days and seeing said spots quite presumptively claimed later by someone's ragged chairs, I began to take corrective action.

For three nights, I went out at 3 a.m. and furiously, however methodically, moved every chair or old bucket or, even, ironing board from my block, deposting each in the alley off my side of the street. I sat in my apartment in the dark till the break of day in hopes of catching the looks on the faces of men and women seeing their parking spaces taken, their chairs magically disappeared. My real hope in this, you see, was that they'd beam happy faces into the cosmos, see the ultimate error of their ways and chalk their losses up to experience. Such, though, had not been the case. I'd yet to catch anyone. And each following day, miraculously, different chairs would be pulled out and used on different parking spaces and the cycle would repeat itself, three nights on.

On the fourth, I came home extremely late after a small get-together with a fellow South Carolinian, an old friend who, over drinks, brought up the subject of our late senator's daughter. My friend thought it all quite laughable, really. He convinced me for the moment. Let us say, then, that my spirits were thus extremely high upon arrival home, so high that a measly wooden chair was not about to block my path to the glee of destruction.

There was nowhere to park, you see, with the exception of a space eight inches deep in snow and in the middle of which was placed, absurdly, its legs deep in the unshoveled snowdrift, a red wooden chair. I wasted no time in harnessing the inertia of my four-door sedan in backing in, tipping and then shattering the chair into a myriad pieces. I panicked—the cracking of the wood had been extremely loud, shattering the Chicago night—and pulled out immediately, rolling down the street to find another space, luckily only a half block from my apartment. I assumed now the chair's owner saw me in the act, that or the big red splotch on the bumper from the contact, prime evidence.

Retribution is sweet release, I thought, standing on the street staring through the empty space where my windshield once was, the dashboard littered with small shards of glass. I scanned the windows of the three-flats lining the block. Might the culprit be watching me just now from an upper window? I pondered my options, ultimately deciding to call off work, after which I visited an auto-glass shop on Western Avenue (driving the few blocks with a 15-degree wind in my face) and spent a heinous amount for the replacements.

We pay for our actions—dearly. Most of us, anyway. Strom Thurmond, with respect to his illegitimate daughter, may have gotten off the hook entirely. Essie Mae Washington-Williams tells stories to television talk-show hosts of traveling yearly to Atlanta from her various northern and/or west-coast homes to meet a representative of the senator who always bore an envelope of cash meant, it can only be assumed in my mind, to keep her quiet. She doesn't quite see it that way. She interprets the cash as "his way" of caring for his estranged child, though Thurmond never actually made the delivery himself, nor did he ever come clean about his siring Essie Mae (who was now in her 70s and no longer any kind of "child").

During the senator's last days—you remember those times, full of mocking news reports of his many gaffes in the U.S. Senate, the man clearly around early adolescence on his journey back to infancy as he flirted with young Capitol interns, even going so far as to grab an ass or two, likewise using the old nasty epithet for the African-American men and women he employed—he saw fit to send only a single birthday card to Essie Mae, signed "Affectionately, Strom Thurmond…" on Senate office letterhead, maybe. I can't remember. The journalist interviewing Essie really wanted to make a big deal of this letter, though I couldn't see that it was, considering that the old man could hardly even put a sentence together during the entirety of his last term, much less a pen to paper. The television journalist must have asked the same question of Essie Mae four or five times in slightly different phrasing—"Do you resent his indifference?" "Does this make you feel slighted?"—trying to get a rise out of her, get her to lay some hatred out on the table. She wasn't going for it. The old lady was promoting a memoir: her personal investment in the ordeal was little at this point; she'd take the money and run on back home, as she'd always done. This was somehow admirable, I thought.

My windshield replaced, I wrote my own note on a piece of hefty cardboard—"Happy, motherfucker?" it read. "We live in a society here!" I even signed it "Affectionately, Strom Thurmond," and camped in my apartment into the wee hours, to the chagrin of my emotionally boxed-in girlfriend, once again to await the curious window breaker, the inevitable "return to the scene of the crime" of urban lore and television cop shows. As I sat through that afternoon and evening, lots of people walked by my car, strategically placed below my third-floor front window. Lots of people read the very large piece of cardboard stuck under the windshield wipers. But none had the look of a window smasher, I figured, and none lingered very long. I fell asleep at an uncertain point propped in the window, the advent of what would be a short, surgical war, but more importantly, a war of shadows, a murky war of words.

Meanwhile, the repeat ascendancy of George W. Bush to the abstract imperial throne approached, and at last the next day my urbane coworkers were engaged in snarky conversations about impending trips to D.C., about their own plans, or lack thereof, for the inauguration upcoming. I remembered my eggy design. But a quick search revealed last-minute ticket prices to have soared if they existed at all, and more importantly I picked up a copy of the *Sun-Times* in a café now just days before the celebration to find a picture of Mr. Bush blown wide across the front cover, the man predictably thin-lipped, his mouth gaping, and I couldn't help but note looking quite like a particular chimpanzee I often visited at the zoo in Lincoln Park, a beast whose name I still can't remember but whom I like to think of simply as Gilbo.

Gilbo likes to stand on his concrete perch and throw things at me when I'm there. Things like banana peels, which the zookeepers give him, I guess, preposterously, and which bounce very anticlimactically off the glass barrier between us. Among Gilbo's other eccentricities are a penchant for addressing visitors such as me as his "fellow citizens," after which he'll go on and say things like "for the last nine days, the entire world has seen for itself the state of our union—and it is strong." And then Gilbo will launch into diatribes in which he very clearly lies to me in every word. He once told me, for instance, that even though his pen in the brand-new Ape House smelled like feces—or more exactly "like a toilet with a large turd floating in it"—things were going just as he expected they should, that the workers, you know, they may have missed a pile here or there, and maybe even failed to spray some of the urine from the corner he used, but you've got to expect these kind of misapprehensivesions.

That word, *misapprehensivesions,* I don't even think it exists, but it's definitely the kind of word Gilbo uses.

At the terminus of his verbal bobbing and weaving I usually point the fact out to him that he is lying, and that I know it, but he just says it's hard work sitting there all day and watching the people come and go on the outside making little baby faces at him when he's got so many grand plans for his followers. "It's hard work being President," says the big ape, using the self-appointed title, as it were. Yes, Gilbo claims dominion over the lot of the zoo's animals. I tell him, typically, to keep thinking, Butch Cassidy, it's his strong suit.

Gilbo doesn't much like it when I come by.

I didn't visit him this day. I had a long night ahead of me at the bar on a stool, where I worked a night a week as doorman. My car had sat all day while I was at the office downtown—apparently the message had not been received. I removed the cardboard from beneath the windshield wipers before driving to the bar, right on glorious Western Avenue, where I spent the night trying to read and getting much of nowhere, my recent battles holding on to a much more prominent position in my mind.

Western Avenue contains absolute mysteries. The road, purportedly the longest perfectly straight road in the nation, bisects my small street just a block and a half to the east of my apartment. The bar where I occasionally work sits on it far south of where I live, as well, and during my late-night trips back north on the road, I have become acquainted with the wonder of an old gentleman who stands at the red light I always catch at Lake Street—he washes the windows of passersby, a gentle wave of the hand is all it takes to wave him off, no need to get angry. But it's what follows that is the ultimate discovery. Try it sometime if you're in the windy city. When the Lake Street red light turns green and your vehicle lurches forward down the nearly empty avenue, Western ceases her normally teasing ways and opens wide, each traffic light flashing to green as you approach just in time for your arrival so that it's possible to end the mile or two north of Chicago Avenue at speeds in excess of 100 mph, if you like, while breaking only a single traffic law. I rarely take it much above 50, and even that's beyond the legal limit—though I figure Chicago cops at 3 a.m. have more important things on the agenda. Donuts. Dealers.

I wonder if Strom Thurmond ever had the pleasure of a drive north on Western at 3 a.m.? Certainly my nemesis has never heard of the old man. That next morning, I woke propped in my window, having replaced the scrawled cardboard message and waiting for the interloper to see it, my gaze instinctively drawn to the specter of my car, whose windows had been spray-painted over in black. Again, there was a note. "hey storm fuck u," it read. I shelled out more cash to have the windows stripped of the paint, filed a police report, and left my own note then in further retaliation, scrawled on a piece of cardboard and secured under the painted-over and nearly destroyed windshield wipers—by then they weren't even needed, though, as the weather had improved to the point that the street was almost completely devoid of snow. My note read, "What do you look like? Sincerely, Strom Thurmond."

The reply came promptly the next morning. "i have brown hair," without this time any retaliatory damage or invective. A dialogue ensued, myself the interrogator, my nemesis the detainee. "Are you fat? Sincerely, Strom Thurmond."

And the answer, in the trademark all-lower-case: "yes very."

"Do you enjoy breaking chairs over your knees like, say, Hulk Hogan or the Nature Boy Ric Flair?"

"very much"

"How often?"

etc…

How quickly simple communication renders warring parties reconciled! I spent my spare time for a few days on the streets of my neighborhood, looking for a pro-wrestler-type, fat, brown-haired man or woman, even, all the while leaving messages, he/she Essie Mae to my Strom Thurmond. Then the final reply came with an attendant blow to the hood of the car, which was dented in. The note, answering my question, "Why do you continue to live? Affectionately, Strom Thurmond," was "i love motherfucker." And that was it. Every further request for elaboration, every further question, went unanswered, and the roles had shifted, the silent treatment the moral equivalent of a prison hunger strike. The Thurmond identity I could no longer claim with any wit or confidence, maybe. I don't know, I got down a little and took a walk down Western all the way to the expressway, by the projects where boys threw rocks at me— I thought all the while of mystery, of the quality of mystery we can expect from our piddling lives. I smoked half a pack's worth of hand-rolled cigarettes on that walk to keep my hands occupied, my fingers freezing in the cold wind where I rolled the last one, on the bridge over the freeway, cars streaming by below, wind blowing in great gusts to the west. The cigarette smoked, I tossed it finally into the traffic. I wrung my hands in the loud silence.

On returning to my apartment, I caught sight of the three-day-old newspaper: George W. Bush on the front page of the *Sun-Times* reminding me of my "friend" Gilbo the chimpanzee. Newspaper photo editors seemed to love running pictures of

Bush mid-bark, right when he delivered some backhanded threat to one of those exotic Middle Eastern countries, his tiny lips pooched out in the middle of a word, mouth wide. I was filled with rage, fear, and hilarity at once. The inauguration scheduled for the morrow, I quickly tramped down to the corner grocery and cleaned out their egg case, then to the copy shop, where I got the Bush head enlarged to a full five-by-five-foot monster poster, which I took home and hung above my fake fireplace.

I stacked the egg cartons along the mantel, where they would have rested through the night until, just at the inception of the oath of office, I would commence hurling egg after egg after egg right into the nose of his enlarged image. But the temptation, I'm afraid, of that imperial or imperious head in half-scowl proved too much to resist.

"What the fuck do you think you're doing?"

This was my girlfriend, walking in at the end of the second dozen—admittedly, the grandiose effect of the Bush-head image was considerably lessened at that point, what with the now-smeared toner, the mess of egg whites and yolks running down the President's chin and oozing slowly off the edge of the mantel, down into the fern in our fake fireplace.

My girlfriend's next words: "Get the fuck out."

She meant it literally, which was unfortunate to say the least. I'd been in the midst of a cathartic release of energy that, cut short, left me feeling quite glum. I made my way with a backpack to the zoo, where I found Gilbo in a state similar to my own, atop his perch picking idly at his nose and muttering to himself when I walked up to the glass. When he saw me, though, he affected a stately bearing, pushing out his chest like a soldier at attention, and intoned, "After the shipwreck of communism came years of relative quiet, years of repose, years of sabbatical."

"Tell me about it," I said. "I just got kicked out of my house."

Gilbo nodded. "We have seen our vulnerability and we have seen its deepest source. For as long as whole regions of the world simmer in resentment and tyranny prone to ideologies that feed hatred and excuse murder, violence will gather and multiply."

"And what of your keepers?" I heckled. I pulled a banana from my pocket and teased him with it from this side of the glass. "Do you propose an insurrection?"

Gilbo let fly a terrific scream, jumped from his perch and banged a fist hard against the glass, then beating his chest once and yelling, "We are led, by events and common sense, to one conclusion: The survival of liberty in our land increasingly depends on the success of liberty in other lands. The best hope for peace in our world is the expansion of freedom in all the world."

I grinned. "That might be two conclusions," I said. He was a sly ape, he was. And freedom, sure, I thought, freedom for all. But I could not discount his implicit specific message, his desire to rid himself of his keepers. It was the first time his talk had chimed with anything close to the truth. Maybe the time of the great ape's grand flourishing, in his walled-off world, was nigh. He banged on the glass again, harder this time, then going down on all fours and menacingly pacing back and forth in front of the slowly rising crowd of onlookers.

Gilbo wanted more.

"The great objective of ending tyranny," he intoned, "is the concentrated work of generations. The difficulty of the task is no excuse for avoiding it."

And the ape went on for over a quarter hour, an astounding outpouring. One man, also accustomed to Gilbo's rants, remarked that it wasn't like the chimp to be so eloquent, so lucid. I remarked that that was partly true, but this was a great gale of wind as well. Gilbo spoke beyond his mettle, of vagaries, "core values" common not only to his oppressed zoo clan but to all living things, a surely preposterous notion.

"We go forward with complete confidence in the eventual triumph of freedom," he said. "Not because history runs on the wheels of inevitability; it is choices that move events. We have confidence because freedom is the permanent hope of all beings, the hunger in dark places, the longing of the soul."

And then he stopped his lurching back and forth and leveled a great stare, solely at myself—yes he picked me from the crowd of gawkers with his eyes, isolating me with the intensity of his gaze, the hair on his back and arms beginning to rise until it would stand fully extended from his body. "And," he finished, raising a fist, "we will never, ever, underestimate our enemies."

With both fists forward he came crashing through the glass and right for my throat, for the world, for us all.

**"Zoo" samples bits of George W. Bush's 2005 inauguration speech.

the stupidist manifesto.

In the monkey economy…insults aimed at us can always be jotted down.
–Viktor Shklovsky

FOCUS on the ape as metaphor for the devolution of man among the urban intellectual set had reached its apex in intensity, far as I could tell, and I think there are multitudes who would agree with me, during the Bush presidency—we're talking George W. here, though I know, I know, we may see another Bush yet, shoot me. I was a woman among men interested, you might say, far before all that, at the end of the Bill Clinton presidency and during Bush's first term, as for much of this time I lived with a couple guys in Chicago who thought they were real literary movementeers, as if that was really even possible in the day and age. There were communities, sure, but those involved seemed to have their expectations in line with the reality of their potential. They knew what they were about, collections of like-minded folks who wanted to stand for something, a primary mode for artists throughout the millennia.

These guys were different. They wanted more than that, be certain, but what that might have been still isn't clear to me, if it was even clear to them. One of the guys, Carl Sealy, like the mattress, could read Spanish and spent time in Mexico pouring over leftist Mexican literature and old surrealist-inspired poetry. Along the way he got hold of Roberto Bolaño's *The Savage Detectives*—Bolaño's not all Mexican, rather Chilean, Spanish, but the book is set partly in Mexico City—long before Bolaño kicked it in 2003 and began to be translated in total. Carl translated parts of it himself for us, the other two in the basement apartment, me and Gervais, whose first name I'm not sure if I ever knew, but he went by his last, in any case. We were second and third command in the corps of something Carl called *La Literatura del Estupidismo*, which translates literally to something like *The Literature of Stupidism.*

We were the Stupidists.

The Spanish was Carl's little nod to Bolaño. The boy had drafted, even, a proper manifesto in the style of the Surrealists or some of the work of Russian futurist and expat Viktor Shklovsky, or Bolaño himself, who had his own famous manifesto—screed of the minor Infrarealist poetry sect in Mexico, early-twentysomethings who in the 1970s straddled the line between the Octavio Paz- and Efrain Huerta-devoted camps of Mexican poetry, populist and avant-garde, right and left or vice versa (though really I think Bolaño was much more interested in no camp whatsoever, which is close to what his manifesto says). *The Savage Detectives* is about the time, partly.

Anyway, on my drive to work the other day—I live in the middle of nowhere east of Tuscaloosa, Ala.—I drove by an incidental convoy headed up a hill on Highway 7 led by a runner in the Guadalupe Torch Run. Carrying an Olympic-type torch in support of immigrants' rights through Cottondale outside of town, the runner led a line of long-haul truckers loaded with steel coils, who inched jerkily along, waiting for him to get the hell out of the way. It struck me as pregnant, the scene's image, perfectly pregnant as antecedent to the long slog of the Chicago Stupidists, less a march in the lead of progress as an unhappy accident that just slowed down other, more ultimately successful runs.

The Stupidist boys were serious, in any case. The thing about Bolaño Carl claimed to admire was the hardcore both/and nature of the author's aesthetic, as he told it. In the throes of the man's narratives you got the sense he was sincerely behind the work, that there was always a lot of emotion in his approach, but also that he was behind the work in a more satirical sense, crafting at a great distance from the subject. Though I have my doubts about how good Carl's Spanish was, it surely helped that Bolaño was always writing about himself, too, a model to fuel the boys' narcissistic impulses.

I don't know why I hung around them.

No, I do know why, or rather I know how it started. Though I'd mostly quit writing poetry by the time I met them, I'd moved to Chicago for that very reason: I would write. I knew there had to be something there that wasn't in Birmingham, old Alabama, where I grew up. In Birmingham we had music, we had hordes of punks with chain wallets, but every writer I'd ever heard of there was a dude in his 50s with a lot of debt and a lonely professor's job. "Go anywhere you like," one of them told me. He was an intro English professor who'd published a novel when he was in his 30s, then languished in a community college I took a few classes at one summer. "Just get the hell out of here, quick as you can."

He hadn't elaborated, but I forever knew he didn't mean just Birmingham but the state, the region. The way he talked about the Old South Disneyland that is Oxford when we read Faulkner's "The Bear" was enough to clue you into how very much he hated the South.

Bolaño says—and I know this because after he died his books were translated, he became an establishment smash, which you probably know, and I got to read them—"Life is a journey toward finding a place to live and work." Something of that nature. No small amount of irony in the construction, but nonetheless most people lose drive and give up before they find their spot. Not me, I found mine, but that's another story. It wasn't Chicago, but the Chi was well worth the shot.

I didn't know at all what I was looking for there, much less what I would find when I left Alabama, but I was pleasantly surprised by the then-dwindling poetry slam scene and tangentially and surely more meaningfully, if that's beyond cliché, a network of more serious writers associated with a few different magazines in town. A couple years into my time there, one of the mags, *Cry*, put on a reading at a fourth-floor gallery space downtown, which I remember distinctly as being odd— Chicago's scene was centered in storefront bookshops, cafés and bars out in the neighborhoods, rough-and-tumble and consequently exciting places with high crime rates and extremely volatile property values, quite unlike the staid old high-dollar buildings downtown. All the same, the neighborhood scenesters were there, among them the Stupidists—it was the first time I saw them—though they weren't calling themselves that yet, in a knot by the windows hanging over Ontario, smoking cigarettes and blasting through the free wine and beer the place was offering, Carl whispering little snickering asides during the readings to Gervais and Kristina Wald, Gervais' Russo-German girlfriend, prompting, alternately, grunts and great peels of laughter at woefully inappropriate moments.

People were looking at them.

In fact, one of the later readers, egg-headed prose experimentalist Ben Marcus, "man without a movement," as Carl later called him, whose stuff I knew and whom I recognized from a reading I'd heard the one time I'd been to New York, turned his bald head and glared at them repeatedly. Carl and Kristina, at least, responded by making silly faces at him. Carl even stuck out his tongue.

By then, in thrall to Marcus' words, amazingly no one in the hall but me seemed to be noticing the exchange. But as the night broke up and guests started talking, everybody passed the word on and got pissed-off and the Stupidists were kicked out, which is I'm sure what they wanted. But not before I got my chance to laugh with them—I'd been dreadfully bored with the scene up until the moment, it was true, and to see Marcus clearly flustered by the shenanigans, worthy as they were of not much more than a sort of high-school admiration or notice, was titillating, or tintinnabulating little bells in the grim night, however you like.

I have the notes I took now ten years later, a horror of lost perspective, to say the least. They chronicle my boredom, if nothing else. The first reader, Joe Wenderoth, who came out with a guitar and read something slurred and slipped through with an utterly pretentious growly thing he did with his voice… Actually, I remember his entire performance much better than all that and, though the entire showing suffered from the guttural quality of the delivery, he well could have been purposefully pushing the audience toward cognizance, apprehension of the then vanguard chimp/ape metaphor, his voice the primary cue to the simian nature of his aesthetic, as the critics are still saying. The Stupidists, I recall—and forgive me for referring to them so abstractly or as a unit, they do have identities, after all, and I was one of them, but to remember Carl and Gervais and Kristina and my time with them is to be launched back into the east-side/west-side gang battle of any old American high school or inner city neighborhood—they were really into Wenderoth at the end of the night, which makes sense in the context of the ape.

In my notes Carl is described as "studly," believe it or not. Skinny rangy dirty longhair Carl is *Studly spindly heckler throws his blue-and-white beer can out the grimy fourth-floor window*. Note the overabundance of adjectives, of detail. For the first time I'd been playing a little with narrative, something I would never master, as you can see. As I was scribbling this, smiling to myself as the local prof, who followed Marcus, droned on a horrible little exercise in poetic futility—the next note immediately following my description of Carl's antics is a terrible line from the poem the prof was reading, *"the crotch of the other is a withered sun,"* or *son?*—I looked up at last and the principle Stupidist caught my eye. He was not smiling at first, but as I bashfully looked away, then back, smiling, a cute grin came to Carl's lips and he mouthed what I took for "This is fucking awful, isn't it?" He was talking to me. My heart fluttered like a little bird in my chest, I am ashamed to admit (I'm usually rather brash, I hadn't had sex for a while, I guess). And though I hadn't been exactly thinking his sentiment, I knew for certain then how very terrible the lot of it all was, the "scene," if this was what passed for it. I looked back to the relatively young prof behind the microphone, both hands clutching the little chapbook he was reading from, his nose aimed down directly into it like we weren't even there, and I stood up and very carefully stepped around and over the seated bodies listening obediently to the prof, on my way across the room to the guys.

Carl and Gervais, he of the single name, formed a perfect Yin and Yang, Carl with shoulder-length curls and a doofus way of exaggerating his points and facial expressions, Gervais looking like a cracked-up version of Morrissey—fauxhawk, horn-rimmed spectacles, smugly serious look on his face when he wasn't harrumphing at his friend's jokes, but he had way too much facial hair; more than stubbly, the man almost had a spiky beard. He was scary, really, but initially I was most attracted to him. Carl just seemed such a mess—and he was, the both of them were, Carl outwardly and unabashedly. Gervais was all sneak attack. He nonchalantly told me that night of his trips to the Cabrini-Green neighborhood, the particular project skyscraper he entered through a doorless hole in the side of the building, a veritable cave in the structure inside which masked dealers plied their trade, after charming the pants off of me with a long bantering back-and-forth about Heidegger and Kierkegaard and etc., etc., the stock-in-trade sensitive boys typically ply, which was somehow refreshing to me at the time. But yes, Gervais was a recreational crackhead and didn't try to hide it. We all had some sort of vice: Kristina was a veritable insomniac who ate shrooms with a mighty passion, Carl drank voluminous amounts of whiskey, and I smoked, I guess. When I was around them I did, anyway.

Long before, and after, I moved into the basement apartment, before and after Carl and I took to regularly rolling around in his little cave of a room, we wrote seated in a circle on the carpet. The sessions were strange. I have most of my notebooks. Carl thought it was destiny that I came along, a poet with a similar sensibility, Bolaño was a poet at heart, La Literatura del Estupidismo needed a poet. We'd brainstorm words for hours—subject-verb or vice versa, adjective upon adjective in a modifier list so long it could quickly cover six pages of a legal pad.

Obsequious, lucid, red, burnt-orange, long, slender, charismatic...

And coming out the end of it we'd write a poem or a story or—something, anyway, sometimes little more than fragment. It felt right, productive, like going to school and coming home with something to show for it—I've been re-reading the un-/finished products lately; they get increasingly angry with time, but at once they're lushly detailed like any overwritten narrative: Stupidist literature.

You'd be surprised, though. Some of them are good. Most are bad. Such is the nature of literature—Carl would say something like that. He did say things like that, forever proposing whatever it was we ended up doing and merely dismissing the failures with pithy remarks about the enduring valor of failure that made him sound smart and vulnerable at once. He was a great politician in that regard.

He's the one, for instance, who proposed staging readings in public parks, which is what the city's denizens probably remember us for if they remember us at all. I doubt they do.

Carl also proposed and mostly carried out the few broadsheets we published, including the manifestoes. La Manifiesto Estupidas, the most important of the ten or so, was a flat piece of paper that could be a poster or could be read like a newspaper on the backside, on the front of which was the mantra of the Stupidists, "WE ARE OUT HERE," borrowed from a local street-theater artist Carl was involved with, followed by a Carl-penned statement of purpose remarkable only for its personal nature, I think, and followed by parodic-serious alternate versions of the manifesto from Gervais, Kristina and me.

But it was Carl's that came closest to sounding genuine, I guess. It was all about him—all self-assertion, assertiveness—in the end. He invoked the ape straight away: *We are the lesser primates among humanity—we require digital extension with pens—but we wear the label proudly, hopefully, forcefully. Apes unite!* He went on to conjure the Bolaño-esque image of the wanderer, the poet-vagabond Carl wanted to be, it's obvious to me now. I guess he was, in a sense, considering his many trips south of the border before we met, though his hometown was out in Berwyn, scarcely ten miles from where we lived, and last word I heard from him he was back there, imaginatively parsing the local population into warring camps on either side of the abortion question in a Stupidist excuse for a novel.

The Stupidist needs not the comforts of home, she draws sustenance from the road, the experience of the new. He then borrowed the Russian Shklovsky's own simian metaphor: *And when in Rome, when immersed in the culture of the humans, the apes live on the rooftops, ever roving, well above the umbrella. The Stupidist is a literatteur for the unsuspecting. We are in the business of the creation of new things.*

The last line was Shklovsky's, almost directly, a trenchant modernist's screed, isn't it. We shouted it at a reading given by an old Chicago confessional poet. We included it in surrealistic or, rather, Stupidistic missives to Mayor Daley we stamped and mailed at the rate of three a week. Not that we ever received a reply. We wheat-pasted our posters all over the neighborhoods.

It never came to a head for me, never blew up or exploded, as I fully expected it would. We got kicked out of plenty of readings, sure, but I waited expectantly for some bedroom argument or a birth, even, a real live birth of a Stupidist baby, no midwife or hospital, just plopped all viscera and sound out onto the sheets of Carl's bed to grow up a monster of American culture. I moved out. I don't remember much. I'd taken a job at a Wicker Park café and could afford my own place. I quit writing entirely. The Stupidists took it out of me, I guess; I lost the energy to withstand the long faces, the frowns of the unsuspecting.

Carl kept me in the fold via email—I rarely actually saw him around. Then my dad died and, back in Birmingham at the funeral, I ran into a lit professor, a different one from my former teacher. This was a guy about my age who'd gone to my college, a very low-level lit professor—in fact he may have been a comp teacher—who in any case knew a lot more about Bolaño than Carl did, and at the same time surprised me after I told him where I was living by bringing up the Stupidists of Chicago. My first thought was that he was a doofus plant, laid there by Carl in a sad self-aggrandizing reach. I'd mostly stopped even thinking about our "movement" by then, it was true. "We are in the business of the creation of new things," the professor quoted, smiling wryly. "That's their ripped-off slogan."

"I know," I said, but he didn't believe me. I didn't elaborate, because, truth is, I wanted it dead, Stupidism dead. It was, I guess, but I wanted the definitive end, the blow-up, because to live and contribute to the decadence at the heart of our culture is one thing, but to it's quite another grow old within that heart as it grows arteries that branch out to supply oxygen to foreign bodies. Without the end, where was I? What was I a contributor to? Where could I remain, safe, free of responsibility?

But I went out with the professor and some others and got drunk and my cell phone buzzed four or five times throughout the night—it was Carl, lending credence to my paranoia. When I called him back three nights later, drunk and mourning at a bar on a Saturday night alone, he gave me a long-winded love letter, essentially. "You don't know what sadness is," I told him—neither of us did. I'd been struck recently by the divergent male/female notions of love and sexuality present in the post-existentialist modernist novel while reading John Fowles' *The Magus*. The men in these novels, inevitably the narrators, want us to think they know better while their women anguish more readily over their lack of commitment. The story was typically their realization that they didn't know anything for certain, and their women were probably smarter than they were. That story is utterly stupid today. Such distinctions are out the window—if anything the reverse might make a great film. *Modern* was just a euphemism for *dumb,* maybe. Dumb women and dumb men at cross-purposes. Today, I like to think we are united in stupidity, not necessarily dumb or incapable of love but senseless with self-love, stupid like the fox.

I won't fall for the romantic bullshit, I told Carl. We are apes at heart, I said, and I think I may have hung up on him.

My sadness was complete as it might be, if it was in fact sadness, mind scattered with my father's ashes, concentration fractured, nonexistent. When I went back to Chicago it was only for a month of packing up and leaving, saying half-hearted goodbyes to my half-hearted friends. They didn't know sadness, either.

I moved to Nowhere, Alabama, outside Cottondale. I study the cultural rippling of the metaphor of the ape's ascendancy in America's perception of itself, the devolution of the population, of the state itself, the slow burn of American exceptionalism and empire alongside the ever-quickening incineration of the world's fossil fuels, the prophetic chimp-mask of George W. Bush's face at the bygone incendiary apex like a paper specter forever glued on the television screen, aggressively sarcastic, nonplussed, full of fabricated wonder, wailing, stupid.

Z's trinity.

THE city was out to get her. The weekend loomed—the third in what we were coming to see as her trio of inevitability. Two weeks prior, after a Saturday party for a bachelorette newly arrived among our ranks, her boyfriend was just off work at a bar in a depressed area of town and drove at our instruction to rescue her not only from a cabal of Chicago Mafiosi at the Redhead Piano Bar but from the bachelorette herself, on the verge of being involved in something none of us wanted, frankly. There were five in the party, in all—Z, we'll call her to protect the innocent, watched her man walk in and, before she could get to him, get collared by the drunken bachelorette, who was, she said, oh-so happy he was there, she and Z would someday soon be sisters ! it was certain, and how happy she was! Well, thank you, the boyfriend said, not realizing the extent to which he'd save the proverbial day, or night, as it were.

We formed a wall between the drunken bachelorette and a salivating, likewise exceedingly drunken, Mafioso who'd been on the verge of lifting the girl from the ground and doing who knows what with her just as the boyfriend walked in. Z, for her part, sighed and then loudly suggested what was on all of our minds—*let's get the fuck out of here.*

And we did, six deep in the boyfriend's tiny Toyota econo-sedan or whatever you'll call it, and after the lot of us were dropped at our respectives apartments, the bachelorette at her less-than-lonely room at the Hyatt, Z and he stopped at a late-night diner, now going on 5 a.m., and were only two or maybe three bites into whatever variety of grease plate they chose to feed the alcohol coursing through their veins when the waitress whined, "You aren't parked in the garage, are you?" like she was mostly disinterested but quite likely holding the knowledge that they were.

"Yes," Z said. "Yes we are."

"You won't be able to get your car for a while," the old lady said. "The garage is a crime scene, it's all taped off."

And the waitress, wide-eyed, disappeared behind the diner's

counter, a hub of activity now as excitement of the news built: Someone had been shot! Oh great day! How wonderful! Other waitresses and waiters and managers and cooks repeated the mantra with something like glee in their eyes—"It's a crime scene! Oh no, you can't get your car now!"—and Z would tell us the next morning at the bachelorette brunch, aka the funereal last hungover free gathering, how she and her man got a cab home and she'd just dropped him off, at noon, to pick up the car, which had been right next to a dark stain on the concrete that could only have been left by blood.

And yet there wasn't by then in her speech any of the abject paranoia that would inflate it in the weeks to come—it was the anger of inconvenience, my God the gall of late-night waitresses and detectives to keep the citizens from getting to their own cars ! private property, etc.

Then the week drew on into the weekend and she was at the YMCA, out in her old west-side neighborhood for her typical 30 minutes on the treadmill, a little light weight-lifting for triceps toning, when she witnessed on her way in an extremely large crowd of loud young men in doo-rags on the basketball court, unusual for a Sunday. She commenced her routine but didn't get five minutes into the jogging when a voice rose behind her, "Is anybody in here a doctor?" She thought of her poor, murmur-riddled heart, and then of the heart of whomsoever it was that had had an attack in the less-than-sterile environs of the west-side YMCA. She thought perhaps briefly of her father and his triple bypass as the voice went on, sounding quite unconcerned, really, "Someone's been shot on the basketball court." The lack of urgency—voice so timid that the import didn't register before her heart fluttered, a delayed beat, an anticipatory surge of adrenalin. "What?" she managed to wheeze.

The owner of the voice now came skittering up to her machine. "No, I'm not a doctor," she said, incredulous but insistent.

There'd been an argument, the man calmly informed her, two young men on one side of it had left, come back right through the front door, and started waving a gun around, at which point their principal opponent in whatever the argument was about—something trivial, surely, a ruling on the court in absence of a referee, a maligned hairstyle—tried to take the gun from the armed man's hands. Z tried to imagine the sound reverberating through the cavernous gym. She could see its back wall, through the window in the gym's second floor in front of her. She tried to visualize the sound bouncing in waves off the 40-foot ceilings and hardwood floor tiles. "He's not dead yet," said the man behind her, "but he's close. Caught him right in the jugular," index finger to the throat.

She was a little happy, at least, that this particular shooting wasn't the end result of a catfight in the women's locker room, for she would be able to gather her things and go. On the way out, after her workout was officially cut short when the gym's manager decided to close early, after the young man's death was official, she was greeted by the specter of a conversation between cops and a woman who appeared to be the deceased's mother. "Only 22," she was saying, completely indignant—she didn't look much over 30 herself. "You motherfuckers won't do shit, will you?" the lady said.

SHE told us this the next Wednesday—how she was convinced the weekend awaited something final, something monstrous—at our typical midweek after-work gathering for drinks downtown. "These things always happen in threes," someone said, and someone else laughed. But not Z. Not I, either. I pledged to be with her this weekend, if she needed the company.

"My boyfriend's acting silly about it," she said. "I think I'll stay in." And she invited the lot of us over Sunday for food and drinks on her back porch. We wouldn't make it as a unit, though. Only I would play witness to the awesome workings of fate.

Sunday was hot. Z had no air-conditioning. On her third-floor porch our sweat was visibly mottling the boards beneath our chairs. And this was an improvement to the sweltering box's insides. Other than she it was me, her boyfriend Ron and one of his friends none of us had expected to see, Jeremy Knowles, a local, very small-time (and small-minded, if you ask me) film-maker who had a penchant for self-deprecating remarks that eventually wound around to deprecating you. Z was visibly miffed by his presence and did her eye-rolling best to ignore him and at once make him aware of it. Knowles and Ron yam-mered on an attempt at an endless metaphor connecting their own filmmaking pursuits to the more glamorous efforts of the hip noise-rock outfits who played in the Chicago clubs. She and I gathered round some plants at one end of the porch and smoked the pot we'd given her Wednesday in concession for [most of] our absence here. "I've never been so superstitious,"

Z said, adding that though she had grown up on the periphery of a smattering of Pentecostals and that there was likely all kinds of speaking in tongues and such nonsense in her extended east-Tennessee Appalachian family. "My mom was a hippie, though," Z said, into stuff like astrology and the spiritual possibilities inherent in psychedelics, that sort of thing—she never fell for the church. Z never fell for either. Acid was an exercise in maintaining control; gave her the willies, like speaking in tongues. Pot was fine, long as the buzz was mild. She cut it with beer and cigarettes, always, she said, finishing off a Budweiser.

Knowles piped in, visibly drunk, "You girls talking about something a filmist oughta be in on?"

"Filmist?" I said.

"I think he wants some of the joint," Z said.

And not that it was malicious, maybe, or even arrogant, but what a douche! Knowles was a waster of the worst type, all the more appalling for his apparent success, the mere fact that he got something done with his time. The boy never combed his hair, went around in the summer in what looked like the same pair of black cut-off corduroys and white T-shirt stained yellow in the armpits. And these outbursts were about the worst, when he was trashed, which was most of the time away from his house, anyway. Not that I'd seen him anywhere but out, though, so maybe I'm being uncharitable.

And we just ignored him, mostly, and Ron for his part seemed embarrassed by the guy—I'd never known them to be friends, I'll admit, and maybe they weren't. Ron kept getting up and moving aimlessly about the small deck/porch and always then ending his vaguely circular amble slumped against the doorframe to the interior, where he'd sort of sway back and forth as if to crank the chattering filmmaker's awareness like a jack in the box, like he wanted the guy to leave.

But of course it wasn't working, and as we all got drunk and drunker—Z brought out a couple chilled bottles of cheap Spumante—Z went on with her talk, she'd never been the superstitious type, really, she meant it, but there was a pattern here that was undeniable. Paranoia is contagious. It crept into me as she broke down the past and possible immediate-future scenarios: 1) a man or woman, identity unknown to Z or any of Z's immediate friends, shot very near to a car in which Z was to be ferried from the place where she was eating, a wall away, really, followed by 2) exactly one week later (if one was to consider the timing of the previous week's killing being in human terms late late Saturday night but in real, mathematically-restricted-by-the-clock terms actually Sunday morning) a boy, named Dante, identity further solidified in Z's mind by the physical sighting of his babbling angry mother, all of which would mean 3) something should happen today, and by her logic it would go down in her proximity and it would involve herself or someone she was well aware of, meaning A) Ron, B) "that fucking jerk Knowles," or C) me.

Knowles heard the last part—I saw his eyes lighting up in glances as Z went on—but egotistically chose to ignore it. I considered the porch, highly rickety as it was. Maybe the coming crisis, like a doom-and-gloom climate change news report, would involve the lot of us in classic Chicago mega porch-death. The papers would eat it up just as they'd devoured the Great Collapse of 2003.

"They're replacing it in two months," Z said, noticing my apparently grim expression, but hammering the paranoia home. If they're just about to replace it, doesn't that mean the probability that it will fall is high?

But I had another small glass of wine and had mostly forgotten to worry, even about Knowles, who continued to run his mouth, sending Ron up and up again to the doorway, back to his seat.

Then I guess no one was really that nonplussed when the first volley came whining over our heads. The sound had been a kind of whistle. I heard it, but thought perhaps a fly had buzzed my ear. The second volley got Ron's attention: he yelped and shook out his hand and, bringing it up to his face, dislodged from the skin of its back a single BB. "Motherfucker," he said, and Z's gaze shot my way, her eyes pinched slit as if the confirmation of her fears was something to rally her focus around.

Just then another volley caught fucking Knowles square in the forehead, and I wanted to hoop and holler in victory, and I did laugh. Z didn't join in at first, but Knowles started screaming—very high-pitched, like a little girl, even—and jumped up to run back into the house when a BB lodged in the flesh of his triceps. Z exploded. We were in tears in seconds. Ron, too.

Across the alley an open window, a curtain half-obscuring the dark interior, was forced closed, and the shooting stopped. Knowles didn't come out immediately, but when he did he was on a mission, demanding to know where the shots were coming from, like we were responsible for them. We pled ignorance, pointing across the alley to indicate the newly closed window but now uncertain of its correct identity—the veritable jigsaw puzzle of the apartment-lined block wasn't about to be solved. By us, anyway. Knowles was determined, and the shots recommenced the minute he got down the stairs, hitting him with uncanny accuracy as he soldiered in an attempt to put the next-door garage between himself and what he thought was the shooter's window. But it continued—a pellet lodged in his wrist. There had to be a second shooter, maybe. Maybe not. We laughed, today, and later, at the happy blessing, another dramatic tale of an eventful life. Death was not in our cards. We were happy.

Arcadia.

I work the desk at the old folks' house, though I also live here. People come in, drug dealers, little high school gangbangers trying to score an initiation sale at the place. They figure a captive audience is all they need. I instruct Benjamin, the 300-pound security guard, to toss them out on their knees. He's always happy to oblige. There's junkies in this place who haven't had a drop of their particular sauce in years, yet they never leave. They need the gatekeeper. They need me.

I met Tristam this way years ago; he turned out differently than many of the little entrepreneurs, though. After a little college at the UIC—that's C Chicago-go, this too-big bootheel of a town—he flunked out, addicted to the city's second letter. He dropped by and was so skinny and haggard I didn't recognize him at first.

"Goddamnit, boy, you look like shit," I said. "Plastic getting to you?"

We went on, as was our style in the days of old, about the plasticizing of the world around us. Plastic car rims, bumpers, plastic cigarette holders, plastic handles on doors to places like churches, plastic communion wafers (taking the symbolic one level higher) slated for reuse—suck and spit, back into the offering plate. Then we struck a deal. Included in my diseased old man's daily dose was a single helping of the groundbreaking Ajexo painkiller. The combination of a Valium-like synthetic with just the slightest twinge of morphine-derivative punch, it was then mythic among the junkie set, regarded as a sort of withdrawal cure-all. I didn't take them no way—I was long off the hard shit and they'd have been a long road back to death for me. Besides, pain I could live with.

In the spirit of God's good grace, I handed them over to the boy. He needed help.

But Tristam didn't keep his half of the deal: staying off the primary jolt. Time goes by and contracts lose their potency. Occasionally I'd start when on the bus on the way to a checkup, a prescription refill, and realize with the full weight of a catastrophe that the boy had gotten off at the park again to see the man who went by Valentino, recognizable by his perpetual attire, an athletic jumpsuit, sneakers, and a fedora over his pristine Afro. The pusher-pimp was known over the blocks for hard shit.

ONE particularly momentous day, I felt like a martyr, like I wanted to be Joan of Arc or some righteous-ass Arab with violence on the mind. Tristam and I rode the bus east on Chicago truly without an idea of what would happen. What we wanted was routine, of course, however chaotic our lives might have been; we could strive. 'Twas all I could do to resist the urge the burn the whole fucking place down, myself with it. For me, the days start nervous.

I keyed the pilot to search the data bank for the right fit. I call it "pilot," but really it's custom, fabricated from the body of an old cell phone. It could get me into any city database long as I had the code. Old girl Jenna Simonsen of the Logan Square halfway house gave it to me in exchange for certain connections only I can provide. John Arbor, Abriel, Arcadia…bingo. I looked to my plastic watch, everything plastic. At 27 minutes past the hour, I ran a background check on myself, Mr. J. Arcadia, to find I'd escaped from prison for the third time, but way back in 1987 more interestingly I trashed the greenhouse of a neighbor in Waukegan, ended up in the hospital and with a charge of indecent exposure on top of other vandalism counts, a two inch gash traveling the length of my buttocks. I got busted with marijuana two years later, and the cops put me in a boarding home with no hope of escape, which is to say without a goddamned chance, much less 12 jurors and a judge.

"There's my money," Tristam said. The flunky pointed to the same park at the corner of Noble and Chicago Avenues, by which we were presently passing. We stood each with one hand gripping overhead poles like chimpanzees, myself keying the pilot in my other hand. The boy was getting bold: Valentino stood there in plain view.

"You mean you're pointing him out to me now?" I said. "What about our deal?"

"Money," Tristam repeated.

"That mean he got money, or he gone take your money?" I said, knowing too well the answer. "Boy, I don't know why you just don't settle on your fix with me. Settle on safety."

"Who are you today?" he said, and before I could tell him about John Arcadia the greenhouse torcher he gestured broadly back west, toward the church. "Meet you there," he said and hopped from the bus, his skinny legs forever appearing like they ought to crumple under the weight of his body, however paltry that was itself. This time he stayed aloft, floating toward the pusher-pimp. And I may have been shaken, distracted or angered by this, and maybe it prefigured things to come, but I didn't get heated just yet over it. I told myself he knew well what he was doing, the fuck, cause I didn't miss a step, headed downtown for my checkup, preoccupied, scanning the pilot for further details.

In 1990, as it happened, I torched a service station, a blaze that singed the eyebrows of many a bystander when it got to the main gas tanks, and did time for it. In 1995 I got out and lit up the prison itself, which ain't here in the record, but I did do it. I'm liberal with history, you might say; the details are there to be eaten and spit back out however you like. Anybody I become picks up this major distinction. They run television commercials about people like me, and usually there is some woman whose voice is over-run with that of a man, and she looks very silly sitting in her posh kitchen at a polished-titanium table talking about the booze and whores she's gonna buy on the vacation she's gonna take to Tijuana on her stolen credit card. I ain't in it for cash reasons, though. Money corrupts absolutely, to modify the old phrase. You might ask Tristam about that one. With me it's more in the blood, you know.

I found a seat finally and just when I got relaxed an old bum strode by and knocked my legs. He was passing out badly reproduced leaflets on which were printed the Lord's prayer. The old son of a bitch stopped just by me and wailed on about the anointed cloths he was gonna give out to anyone with any bit of change whatsoever. He yelled through the bus, erupting brash and ugly in the center of this morning commute; everyone ignored him but me. I could be him too, and was excited at the prospect for the moment, for I knew there would come a day when the pilot stumbled upon the fate of all gadgets of its kind, broke, and left me hanging with a story I couldn't play for keeps. I needed another option.

I asked the bum his name. He looked a little like me. He stopped his sermon and turned my way, his eyes going wide. "My name is your name, Jehovah," he said, which I promptly keyed into the pilot. "Jehovah," the old bum repeated. The bus slammed to a hard stop, the vagrant swaying with the tide. Yeah, I could be this guy. "Last name, social security," I said. The bum's eyes shot wider still, and he broke into the prayer on his mangled photocopied leaflets, holding one up close to his farsighted eyes and shuttling out the rear door in the same motion, midsentence, at Larrabee. On his way out he dropped one of those "anointed cloths" he was talking about. Before anyone else could get their hands on it—it was bright blue, a pretty picture against the ribbed black rubber of the bus's floor—I jumped. It's a holy day, I figured. I remained standing in honor.

They were gutting the old Montgomery Ward building at the time, turning the commercial space into luxury condos. I could look out the bus's windows from my spot and see straight through the 20 and some floors of the monstrosity. Can't break a structure that solid, been standing much too long now, and the developers figured it to go the route of the rest of the neighborhood south of Chicago this far east since the retailer shut down, absolutely fucking filthy rich. It wouldn't necessarily work out: on the north side of the street of course sat the outer edge of Cabrini-Green, the minuscule streets dead-ending before Chicago Avenue in cul-de-sacs, the single-story brick boxes reminding me of projects in cities much smaller. Say Charlotte, Atlanta. Long time since I'd seen those places.

I got off the bus at State and trekked it two blocks south to the clinic for my checkup, then down to the old-school pharmacy on Superior to refill my many prescriptions. I left feeling truly like a savior in spite of the name on my health card—Arcadia I am not. I pulled the blue cloth from my pocket and brought it to my nose. It smelled like the bum, stale and musty, slightly sour with sweat and urban rot. But hidden deep in that stink was a sweet flower blossoming. I could be Jehovah or any other body. Not like there was somebody to tell me different.

Like you, I am dying a slow death. Jehovah is not dying, nor John Arcadia though he could have at any moment thrown himself into the molten steel at the Gary Works in Indiana—keeping close to mind of course his proclivity for self-destruction, for fire. But we are all sick; just listen to the wind roaring in our ears, here.

My prescriptions took up a ten-page stack of printouts from the doctor's dot-matrix printer. The pills came prepared in a plastic, slotted box, one small compartment to correspond to each day of the coming month. I do not know how I managed to keep up with them—Jehovah the meek, the persecuted, the resolute, the vigilant? I gazed up at the time on a digital display clock outside the Holy Name Cathedral, then at my plastic, everything plastic, watch and made my way to the next meeting, muscling to the back of the bus, pilot switched off in my little drug bag. Today, I would need it no more. My name was secure.

I was spot on time to the old abandoned church, where I spent my nights and many days besides before the old folks' home took me. Tristam wasn't there. I took my day's meds sitting on the concrete steps before the boarded-up space where the door used to be. I had been waiting for the kid for nearly an hour when the nausea and pain kicked in and I crept through the space between the half-kicked-through boards and laid down in the dark of the vestibule in communion with the saints, the wind and whine of the expressway now a fading memory, nothing present but the pain; I concentrated, pinpointed all my holy energy on a flash behind my eyelids and soon enough fell fast asleep. When I woke the nausea was still present but the pain had subsided. "Tristam," I called out, expecting the kid to be conked there somewhere near me in the dark. There was no answer, but I listened and could hear above the low outer din his breath coming in long, slow gasps. "Motherfucker," I said, crawling dazed toward the sound. Nothing. I punched what I took to be his leg, and a voice I didn't know boomed calmly through the dark.

"Who are you now?" it said. I got to my feet.

"Jehovah?"

Then a scrambling broke out and I was forced down onto my back, tackled. Tristam laughed through the darkness. "Gotcha."

"Goddamnit boy," I said. Tristam giggled and giggled on, and when finally I got a look at him, when he turned the flashlight on and I could see, I divined in the glare on his eyes that he was fucked.

"I was just kidding, old man," he slurred. "Don't look so damn mad. You got the shit?"

"I'm holding," I said.

"Oh ho ho. Well hand it over."

"I mean, you ain't getting anything until you hold to your side of things."

He sorta held there, held the flashlight pointed upward, held his body tensed in that brief attempt at comprehension of my words. And then when he fished through the muddled bank of connotations and meanings in his head, when he got what I was saying, I guess, he lunged at me, raising the flashlight high in the same motion as if to bring it down on my head. I caught his hand and any fear the young man may have mustered in my head quickly turned to righteous rage. I wheeled out the only thing of particular strength I had anywhere near, the pilot, and in the gloom wheeled it around and caught Tristam on the side of the head. He fell hard to the ground, the flashlight rolling from his hand and coming to rest with its beam shining right in my face.

"You never wait for me to answer," I said. "What's my name, motherfucker? What is it?" He didn't answer. "You call me Jehovah, you hear? Jehovah."

I crawled over him and brought the pilot down on his head again and again and again. Tristam didn't move. I may have hit him ten times, twenty times, but I know I stopped, the pilot now an unrecognizable mass of cracked plastic, everything plastic, and other parts. I crawled into the sanctuary, where the light penetrated the empty window spaces above, lighting on the old wooden altar, where I knelt and prayed for the first time in years, through it all the murmur in my head telling me that the fraud of the act was just that, a fraud, that I was praying to myself, that I alone would determine the route to salvation.

A week or so after I killed the boy I stepped up on the bus, strident in my conviction, noble as the street itself as I paid the bus driver, murmuring "God bless," and turned to face the crowded interior.

"I am Jehovah!" I hollered.

I opened my bag, bowed, and flung a handful of baby-blue towels into the crowd. I pulled a flyer up to my eyes and began to read, "Our father, who art in heaven, hallowed be thy name…"

Jim Threatt's crisis of faith.

Then I saw an angel coming down from heaven, holding in his hand the key of the bottomless pit and a great chain. And he seized the dragon, that ancient serpent, who is the Devil and Satan, and bound him for a thousand years, and threw him into the pit, and shut it and sealed it over him, that he should deceive the nations no more, till the thousand years were ended. After that he must be loosed for a little while.... —Revelations 20: 1-3

WHEN I got work at Flix Auto back in the late 1950s I did not have any foreknowledge whatever about the existending philosophy. Clyde Flick, my boss, taught me all about it. "The French didn't have nothing to their credit this century excepting the paltry legacy of their booze," Clyde told me one sunny day. "They were whipped twice soundly by the Germans and we had to go over there and save them. But then they came up with this: life don't mean two shits. You'd think they'd figured it out after the first war, but it didn't truly take hold till the second." Clyde himself might have been a Frenchman but for the fact of his talking to my mind like a West Virginia hillbilly, the short little man quite out of step with the most of his Scots-Irish kin, big men raised up in Forest City and beyond, up in the North Carolina hills.

He had more in common with one in particular, though, who lived just around the corner from Flix by the college, the diminutive literature professor Hank Ledbetter. "Hank told me all about it," says Clyde. "They got their smart ones together over there and finally someone in the world had the balls to confirm it, for the record. Books and books written on it, printed and all—it's all one big steaming ball of horse manure, this existence. I even got through one of the books myself."

Clyde was a squat old man with a rat's face and no hair who came down to my town here in South Carolina via Charlotte and a moonshine run back in the 1920s, I think, when he was 17. I'd come to admire him for this thinking. He was good at it, a good deal better than me, in fact, though my Pop always did say I was the thinking one of the family. I was seven when I rebuilt my first Ford. Pop Threatt didn't even really have to tell me how it was done, just that the idea was to separate the block out from the rest and then refit the total package to a more exact thing that it was prior. Things get loose and go bad over time, he said. So I pilfered some of his tools late one night and started it while he was sleeping. He was piss-mad the next morning when he had to walk to work, but two weeks and several visits to a scrap yard on, the job was done, and that 1940 coupe was purring smooth and fierce like a tiger.

But Clyde Flick of Flix Auto was far above me, thinking up there in the clouds where my head gets all befogged trying to wrap itself around any idea, really.

Flix Auto used to be a feature movie theater, the first one the town ever did see. We did not use the theater portion, though Clyde had expressed dreams of gutting it of all the dusty old chairs and rigging it with new lights, leveling the floor, turning it into a regular warehouse garage, high and quick turnover like the ones they got up in Charlotte. I laughed when he told me stuff like this. "Keep thinking, Clyde, keep thinking," I said, which got him red hot, typically. The operation here was just me and him in a little patch, half paving and half dirt, that used to be a drive-up at the front of the theater. A makeshift wooden plank tacked on in place of the old marquee out front was our covered garage, though the sign by the road still said F — L — I — X in big fancy letters, the old "theater" crossed out and replaced with the brush-painted "garage." We worked on the cars there, checking people out in the lobby, which was still made up like it's 1929, a busted chandelier hanging high up over the counter and rattling in the draft that rushed through the place, giving cause to folks to sneak worried glances up into the high tile ceiling while they pay.

"The fear of death is about the only thing that will lead a man to pay what he owes," Clyde once told me. He had no fear himself, of course. I'd say it's cause he held the key to the register, though he'd tell you the existending philosophy did deliver him from trepidation.

"I told Hank," Clyde said, "I told him when he showed me them French books that I'd figured this shit out long ago. Life is two shits but going about your business, whatever that may be, fixing cars, bringing in the cash to buy the toilet tissue and the corn on the cob that sustains and keeps free of shit the sticky lifeblood of us all." The trick, the old man believed, was figuring out how to face that simple fact without blowing your damn head off at the stupidity of it.

"What about Jesus?" My perennial question.

I was raised a Methodist and, God willing, I will die one.

Clyde didn't believe that for a second, Jesus was something he made up to tell his kids when they themselves turned 13 and began to comprehend just how stupid going to the store and buying toilet tissue and soap and pork chops was.

But his talk still couldn't explain what I seen with my own eyes, which I am getting to presently.

CLYDE believed the white man's hatred of negroes was along the same lines of belief as Jesus, which is one of those high-flying things I can't quite get my head around. "It don't mean shit," said he, bald head glowing fire red like every ounce of blood in his body had congregated in his skull. Tire iron in his hand, poking at the air with it like it's a weapon, he'd go on to call the hatred "a worthless and stupid thing made up for the benefit of an ass-poor hillbilly, like for instance my older brother Charlie, back up there in the hills. The man has nothing but bright pure love for his disgusting ugly wife. The sight of her would take paint off a house, it's a fact." Charlie, said Clyde, had one other dubious monument to his pride. "The fact that 'God made him better than the niggers,'" he said. "If that ain't a load of shit I don't know what is." I tended to agree with him, frankly. Some make up Jesus, others make up the beauty of their wives or the grace of their husbands, and others, well, they look around for a face that's a different color and figure that face for an idiot's, which keeps them going full bore on a trail toward some kind of salvation. And it's a man's prerogative to believe what he wants, I guess, but at the time Clyde told me all this I thought the best way to test the man's contention was to meet them Freedom Riders coming out of Charlotte in April that year. I heard about it on the evening news. Came off less like a news report than an announcement, really, a strange kind of warning. The riders were due in right at noon, said the lady on the television, though I swear I detected a crazy gleam in her eye, like even she couldn't wait to see what would happen when them boys tried to enter the Greyhound station's whites-only waiting room. They'd been doing it all through North Carolina without incident, she said. The lady seemed to be blinking a little cockeyed, almost winking, through the whole damned report.

I suppose I should have confirmed it there, took her spastic eyelids as a yes, a gang would come out and show me clearly that my boss Clyde was right, that life and Jesus and all was worth less than three runny shits out a car window, like the hatred of the men. But I went out there anyway on my lunch break, stood outside the waiting room and watched them all there through the window. There were about 20 men in the white little square of the waiting room, waiting. They wore short-sleeve blue oxford shirts and workpants. Looked like a lunch shift straight from the bleachery where my father had worked. They stood in the room and passed cigarettes around and didn't bother to chat with the lady at the Greyhound counter nor talk amongst themselves to at least put up the appearance of men waiting for a bus. They propped their arms on their knees in various seated and leaning position, cigarettes stuck smoldering in their teeth, all eyes aimed at the door.

About that time a lone man, rather a spiffy black boy in a suit and top hat, came down off the big silver bus and waltzed straight up to the door. The men didn't make a move. I took the time to kindly remind the black boy he wasn't supposed to go in there and that if I was him, I wouldn't. The boy just adjusted his necktie, though, wiped some sweat from his brow, shot out his chest like a soldier and said, "I am guaranteed by the decree of" such and such, for that was what them Freedom Riders were up to, testing some Supreme Court declaration. I put my hands high and backed away. "Don't say I didn't warn you," I said.

The boy nodded sternly to me and walked right up to the door.

I could feel the fluorescent hatred in the bleachery men's eyes burning me through the glass. The one that greeted the black boy was himself a boy, skinny as a rail and outfitted with a ratty white undershirt, his hair all mopped back with pomade like a country hick trying to look like he belongs somewhere important. He was likely the youngest of the pack.

"Where you think you going?" he barked to the well-dressed black boy, who chimed in with that same declaration he had done given me.

"Aw no," the country kid said, "you ain't coming in here."

And he spat right on the black boy's nose.

"Hey, wait a second!" I said, but the ratty white kid glared at me—something in his eyes flashed, like suddenly the black of the pupil had overtaken his blue irises and the whites too. The black boy hadn't seen it, I don't think, his eyes on the crowd off the little hick's back, for he repeated, "I am guaranteed by the act" of such and such while pulling his handkerchief from the pocket of his sport jacket and wiping the spit carefully from his nose. The little hick didn't say a thing, just came out of the doorway now and pushed the black boy back on his heels and then flat down on his butt. I backed away, eyes flashing under benches and around trees, wondering where the poor kid's friends were, hoping another dark-faced soul would come and save the poor bastard. And when I looked back to the waiting area the men were blowing out the door and beating on that black boy with their fists and brogans. The little hick, though, he stood at the back of it all, leaned up against the brick of the station smoking a cigarette like nothing was going on, half-satisfied look on his face.

I'd seen enough—had had about enough of the kid's bullshit, and I was a good deal damn mad, knowing I was beat, the Great Lord damned and no more than some halfwit prevaricated by the middling fancy of an auto mechanic or old Hebrew soothsayer which, I figured in that instant, were just about one in the same. I puffed my cheeks like a toad before I said, "Hey!" and marched over to the little hick with a mind for I don't know what.

The boy sucked on his cigarette. "Howdy," he said, and his eyes flashed black again. His nosed seemed to grow an inch or two and point itself right at my face, combining for an instant with his mouth. Then, with a distinct rush of air, upward, he was gone, though he might have fallen into a hole for all I knew—it happened so quickly. His cigarette was left smoldering there in the dirt where he'd stood.

The police showed up some time later, and I heard tell a bunch of those bleachery men were arrested. But I was long gone at that point.

I drove back toward Flix Auto and my ratfaced boss who, not taking into account the hick, I had to figure, was correct in thinking hard to the conclusion that the Great Lord Jesus was nothing but a made-up thing in the collective mind of a pack of racist factory workers, all went off like so much clockwork. I drove my Ford and thought on the existending philosophy of

Clyde Flick, wheeling the car down these straight town roads and thinking hard despite the fact of the beak I'd seen spring right out of that kid's face like he was some sort of alien thing. I was turning onto Elizabeth off Main, though, when there come a loud thump on the roof of the car. I pulled into the parking lot of the Episcopal church and got out. Sure enough—a big dent center forward of the roof. I got mad, a little, looked out across the road for kids throwing rocks, as there weren't many trees to speak of, when came a voice right at my back. "Hello, Jimmy!" it boomed, like it was right in my ear. I wheeled around, bracing my back against the car, to find that little hick just a few yards off, by the road, hair still slicked back and greasy with pomade and his shirt now dirty like he hadn't had a bath in weeks.

I pressed myself more securely against the car. "Who the hell are you?" I demanded.

"Jesus," he said then, his voice a strange approximation of redneck and something other. He sounded much older and Yankee, like old tapes of FDR or maybe that crazy McCarthy. "Jesus Flick," he said, twitching a little like he had an itch on his nose.

"Flick?" I said. That was a lie. Clyde had changed his name from Ledbetter—it didn't mean shit no way, did it—just to take advantage of the old sign at the abandoned movie theater when he'd bought the space. "You ain't no Flick," I told the hick. "And no one walks around calling himself Jesus without something to show for it." The kid did not look Mexican to me, either.

But he seemed then to cave in on himself, his chest bulging up under the white shirt, his stomach sucking in. "You're right," he said now, spitting into the maybe ten feet of space between us. His pupils overtook the rest of his eyes, the black holes then narrowing down with a leathering of his eyelids. His nose come out on itself in a beak, combining with his mouth, his ratty shirt puffing up a little more about the chest like a feather pillow and his arms sprouting feathers themselves.

"Good God," I gasped, leaned hard now against the car door. I nearly did fall. The boy, the thing, rather, took on the character of, say, a bird, or more exactly a walking-tall turkey, complete with a sagging outcropping of flesh that hung like cooked collards from his chin. He spoke in that old crazy Yankee voice now, saying, "No! No sir! I am not a Flick! But my name is not of your concern. Ask any of the boys down at the bleachery and they'll tell you no differently. It serves their dumb heads not to know it. If they did they might renounce the Good Lord like you have done, Jimmy."

How he managed to get the words out of his beak I do not know, likewise how he knew what I was thinking. I tell you it scared me. I turned my back to the unholy sight to get into my car and this oozing, half-animal voice came out of the thing now, saying, "Stay awhile. I've got things to tell you." Turning back, I saw he'd changed back to the skinny hick he'd been before, the slick hair, his white undershirt as if stretched to the breaking point and set back again, which I guess it had been. I stood there and stared hard at a soiled spot on the shirt at the left shoulder, not hardly even thinking a thing. I slumped against the car and waited for whatever was next. I watched the shirt, then after a time indeterminable now to my mind I let my eyes run up his shoulder to his face, and what I saw was that the boy looked sad now, not sassy or mean or even stupid.

"You like them Pall Malls?" he said. I coughed, then told him I didn't smoke much but I had to figure Chesterfields would be my brand of choice.

"Well," he said, "I like the Pall Malls. To each his own, I guess. The fact does remain that I am out." He pulled from a pants pocket a twirled-up empty pack and threw it out into the road. "And I don't much feel like walking today. Mind giving me a ride?"

Fear had me stupid, I guess, cause I let the turkey in my car and drove down to the filling station where he bought himself a pack, instructing me to wait. He owed me, he said, and when he plopped back in the car he passed a pack of Chesterfields across the console. "I don't normally encourage a man to smoke," he said, "but you look like you need it."

I lit one and it tasted damn good despite the early April heat, summer coming just around the corner. We sat idling and I did burn the whole stick before, a little woozy, I pulled out. The boy directed me to a little diner on the road toward Charlotte, a dump of a place called Vic's where he seemed to fit right in. The men at the counter, farmers or truckers or whoever they were, all shook his hand in a row when we came in. We sat in a booth next to the windows facing the road, ordered coffee and sat staring at each other for a time. After the second refill, with the greased-up hick staring at me silently through it all, I was so hopped up on the thick brew that when the waiter called out the boy's named as "Rolly" I could take the suspense no longer and said, "So what is your name, then?"

"My name is not of your concern," said the hick, "though your obsession with it is altogether common. I was sent to teach you something. Your boss, for one, has it all wrong, but it ain't his fault. We like to blame it on ourselves, the Kennedys, and not your President nor any of them Senators-to-be, for they were sent on a different mission. Theirs is not His—" here the boy pointing upward into the smoke-stained ceiling of the diner, sipping his coffee with a quick gasp before going on: "Good people, some of us might be, though it's only lately that we've had to take on such despicable roles as the one you saw me in back at the terminal." His eyes looked away from me now, out into the highway, and in them there lay that dreamy sadness I'd seen back in town by my car.

I was twitching now from the coffee. It leant the kind of feeling a sick man may have for his dog, or a sobering drunk for his poor beaten wife. He seemed to be damn sad, and I told him so.

He turned his black eyes back my way. "My name is Ephestus Kennedy," he said, "if you must know. It's a long line we run. You people have seen us before, though we've been relegated to the dustbin of unrecorded history. We helped burn your towns last century and then returned afterward posing as doctors and such—good, civic-minded folks bent on saving you, all cause you'd gotten on the wrong path from the beginning, slavery and the exaltation and mistreatment of the women among you and drunk on your own richness on plantations and with wrong-headed, positively evil ideas. We didn't recognize how very obstinate you would be. Our focus was battered. It got so bad that here we are retracing steps from the center—with the evil negro-hating men you saw at the bleachery, likewise the other side of that fight.

"The nature of belief," continued Kennedy, "says to the man who holds it that all the other side's stuff is nonsense, but the other side thinks the same thing, essentially, which makes them equals, see. What has happened here, and your despicable boss is absolutely right on this count, is that two things, one ugly, one His," the boy pointing again into the ceiling, "His own great single truth, have gotten inextricably tied up, and I'm here to play the two sides against themselves, which might sound diabolical, and maybe it is, but play party to both sides, nurture belief, wrong-headed or not, thus pumping each up like a damn flat car tire, and what should result is harmony, after the clash.

If it all goes right, if you don't start accepting the far gone and devilish wisdom of your northern cousins."

"But frankly," the boy went on, not a smile anywhere near his mouth, "I'm jealous—jealous of the others. Their roles are bearable, on the other side."

I just watched the boy, now for the moment unable to speak to anything he'd said, afraid to, and Ephestus Kennedy lit another cigarette and his hand shook the match out violently. I lit one myself to fill the silence, and tried to begin to really wrap my head around what he was saying. All the while, the boy's body began to shake like my caffeine-addled limbs, but more violently. I think he was struggling against what was happening. The change was under way.

His fingernails grew, extending and curling right around the coffee mug he was raising to his mouth, which bulged, elongated into that beak-like state. He puffed on the smoke. I brought my own cigarette to my lips and shielded my eyes against the sight with trembling hand. "This is our true form," I heard. And a sound like paper tearing came from inside the turkey. "It is disgusting, ugly," Kennedy said.

I chanced a long look out into the gloomy diner and all was as normal—three men sat at the counter smoking, drinking coffee. One had even turned this way, but it was like he simply didn't—or couldn't—see what was happening here. The big smoking turkey was fidgeting now with something under the table, his claw coming up with a little pistol fixed in it, which he pointed at his head. His breath came in quick, hard gasps. "Keep the good faith, Jimmy," he wheezed. His black eyes, if I could even read them, looked to be searching me for something—something that wasn't there, I'm afraid, for he pulled the trigger and splattered the front windows with pomade-greased feathers and blood and left the boy's body slumped in the booth. If that turkey were his true form, Ephestus Kennedy, Rolly, Jesus Flick, whatever, he did die a lie.

"YOU were right," I told Clyde when I got back to Flix that night, after of course him laying into me with all the vitriol the little man could summon for being gone all afternoon, though he was probably more upset about the dent in the roof of my car, an automobile which he himself had worked on for years, including a great deal of body detail, before bequeathing it to me.

"Right about what?" he said.

"Let's fix this damn dent," I said. "Then we can maybe roll over to Main and get a few beers."

"Sounds good," Clyde said, and we began working out the dent. I thought on to myself that it all may well have been a phantom thing but for the dent, which Clyde would expert out of the old car, surely. And I asked him about the French as we worked, and he banged his hammer at the roof and explained it all over again, but I lost the thread of his nasal whine after a time and set my sights on the dent, which was losing its prominence by the minute. I focused hard on it, for a dent in the roof of a man's car is something one can get one's head around, and I will forever refuse to take such a thing lightly.

fish camp gamers.

JO'S Fish Camp sits next to a vacant yard on its left, on its right a textile mill that extends about half a mile up Main and butts its old brick flush against the grounds of the bleachery, where me and Louie worked.

"Got five?" Louie said.

"Five what?" I said.

"I feel like hitting the camp today," he said. I took it he meant dollars for Jo's greasy catfish plates, though time might have been something to think about. We ride our lunches well past their predetermined end, talking of the jet-black girl I let get away—we both let get away. Louie's white, but 20 years on he can't get her out of his thick head. Every day for the past two weeks, we've hit the camp for the lunch hour, drunk our minds silly courtesy of Jo's new liquor license, and talked like two old fogies with nothing on their minds but death.

It had gotten out of hand, a little. Two days ago, the foreman, super on the shift, me, almost got fired for my inability to keep it to myself. On the pretense of borrowing a cup of coffee from secretary-to-the-boss Annie's pot, I lingered too long in the boss's office. I stood way up over Annie's shoulder, asking her what she was doing, and I got caught up in the perfumed scent of her red hair, my eyes rolling way back into my head at the beauty of it. Oglethorpe couldn't have seen much when he came in, just me standing behind Annie. But at once, a thick tendril of drool emerged from the just-open corner of my lips quite unbeknownst to me. It dropped slick and slippery on her arm, and I knew I'd fucked up.

"You drunk bastard! Goddamn no-good monkey bastard!" she screamed, and I compounded the problem by laughing, of course, while she ran off to the bathroom.

Oglethorpe stood right there through it all. "My goddamn foreman," he said. "Drunk. It's a travesty!" Oglethorpe could hold his own with all the old filthy-mouthed comedians, from Bruce to Murphy to Rock. He adjusted his tie and rolled his neck a little, huffed through his nose like an angry bull. I backed out of the office.

Louie sauntered up wagging his head back and forth like to say, I can't believe this old boy getting drunk even at work. That's exactly how it came off—a promotion plea in solidarity against me, but I know it's just Louie giving the old man a swaggering chance to make a fool of himself. But Oglethorpe didn't fall for it. "You," he said, "you dago son of a bitch. What do you think of your boss getting drunk on the job?"

"I ain't drunk," I said.

"Shut up, White," Oglethorpe said, his gaze never leaving Louie. "Let the man speak."

Louie's hand went up like a schoolboy's. "Actually, I'm Irish, sir," he said.

I nearly fell down with the force of the laughter booming through my body, but Oglethorpe didn't take to our man's talking out of turn. "What the fuck ever, Murphy, I know you're Irish. Wipe that silly look off your face. You drunk too?"

And the boss must have come to a quick decision to leave it alone, for he wheeled around like to walk away, wagging his head back and forth in ultimate disapproval, muttering "goddamn imbeciles," but leaving nonetheless. That wasn't enough for the white whale. Louie decided to answer the man's question. With a small grin my way, he uttered just the one word: "Quite," he said.

Oglethorpe wheeled around and said something very angry-sounding now, but I wouldn't make it out, only a tear-blurred sight of his face, red like on the verge of combusting. He stormed into his office. I heard him through the walls, then— dago this! Nigger that!—and Annie's protests to him to just leave us be, the sweet old lady.

That's two days gone now.

I call Louie little, but he's about twice my size. I guess it's my years that give me cause—I've got almost ten on him.

I told him I'd afford his $5 lunch if he'd let it stop there, lunch and a beer, and not his typical "four for a couple more." Jo's liquor license doubled the price of the lunch hour for both of us. My wallet had taken a big hit from two weeks of this.

The little bell rang for the first lunch shift to cut off and, like clockwork, we sifted into the sunlight, floated up the road past the mill and into the old wood door at Jo's. The handle rattles in your palm as you push on it, before you zig-zag your way through the maze of tables inside.

We sat as always against the wall in a booth that looks beaten, straight out of a failed pool hall. Jo's got it shoved up against the rear plaster like he's not planning on giving it a chance to ever feel at home. The seats are gaudy red, curved to fit your ass but they don't. The tabletop's a fake formica thing, white vinyl covering peppered with little gray squiggles and bordered by an aluminum ring.

"Hey Jo, get a coupla beers over here?" I called out to nothing. Who knew where the old man was? Back someplace stroking his pointy pirate beard, maybe. He'd bring the beer out soon enough, though.

I say two weeks, but it's more like a decade we've been sitting around jawing about the girl, Dedra, my then-girlfriend. Fifteen and some years together and she up and left me for a banking man, probably sits right now on the stoop—balcony, more like—of a Charlotte skyscraper apartment building sipping on a martini or something. She knew what she wanted, at least, Dedra—the big black girl that our little white boy, my now quite large friend Louie, couldn't get out of his head. So he stormed straight from his second-grade classroom, posted up right in front of his house at the end of the walk from his front door. He sat three hours straight then in the hottest sun yet that year, knowing Dedra would be swinging down the road within striking distance on this very sidewalk, after being released from her own late high school class.

Dedra—tight cutoffs, tree-trunk thighs, late-spring sweat putting a shine all down the round backs, what little Louie wanted.

"So bad, J., so bad," Louie telling the obvious. I slumped in my seat, watching his shaggy head as he did the same. Jo appeared above us, leaning in to wipe the table with a half-hearted circle, plopping down two beers. "Bad, bad cravings," Louie said. "Damned awful horrible."

"Two catfish?" Jo said. We nodded.

"You were so young, though," I said—despite the fact I've heard this story a million times, and that I was there, I still find the memory a little difficult to swallow.

"Crazy early puberty," Louie pulling back on his can and rising now, following Jo back to his spot by the register, where he asked for the checkerboard. We blew through four or five quick matches in silence, him trouncing me, as usual—Louie black, J. Red—until my fingers bled from the thinking.

"I had pubes when I came out of the hole," Louie said. Here he kinged one of his blacks with the only casualty I'd managed to retain this match. "Had a peach-fuzz stache at age five. Shaving by seven."

"Torn up at nothing but ten by a woman!" I said, "a damned girl, even." Then I couldn't stand it no more. "Alright, that's enough," I said, sweeping my arm across the board and sending the checkers cascading red and black down to the tile floor, where they clattered, bounced, warranted a "What the fuck!" from Jo back behind the register, a genuinely pained expression from Louie.

"Now what'd you go and do that for?" He leaned over and out of sight below the table to begin picking through the casualties of my latest act of violence. I couldn't help it.

I picked up my spoon and began tapping it on the table's aluminum ring. I turned up my beer and downed it in a gulp. "Hey Jo!" I said. "How bout a couple more here!" I do get sick of losing.

HE wanted it so bad, Louie, that he'd lost the ability for a time to focus enough to beat even his stupid little brother at checkers. Came to a point he sat waiting for Dedra all afternoon, skin rising on his pasty-white face and arms in sunburn welts, out front of his house, one of only two white boys on the block—the other his brother—and I was waiting for her, too. After I dropped out I'd always be there, out front of my little place three doors down from Louie, waiting, long as it wasn't a swing-shift week, in which case I'd be down at the bleachery hoping for fire and flood both before a jam-up of the machines, not much is new.

Blazing hot that day. Me and Dedra'd been spending her after-school time skinny-dipping down at Pete's Landing, owned by a friendly old man who gave us kids the run of the place. Hottest day yet that year, the leaves of the trees lining the road washed full out of color. Late May, school almost out for everyone and me and little second-grade Louie separately tapping our feet, rubbing our own shoulders as they burned in the sun, waiting.

I puffed my smoke and had been watching little Louie for

half an hour before I looked up the road again, up by where he sat about half a football field along, and here she came. Queen Dedra—hips swinging back, forth like the pirate boat at the county fair, the black of those thighs shimmering even in this bland light. I tossed my cigarette back up in the bushes—she chastised me for the habit, even at 19. I gazed up the road. She swung along, hot and slow, undistracted by little Louie sitting eagerly directly in his path, drool threatening to slip from the corners of his mouth, tongue lolling out—much like my own state, Louie's, tantalized by the swaying of this picture-perfect woman. She swings this way, catches me looking and raises a hand up level with her chest in a sexy wave. Swaying, coming on slow to Louie's spot by the sidewalk. She has stopped now, hitched, rather, for it ain't a full stop, really. The hand is up in a wave and she is smiling, but what I'm seeing is the dive, the forward thrust of Louie's gleaming white face, mouth open, teeth bared and tongue out and all pitching forward into the back of Dedra's left thigh. I wished I had a camera: Louie in the instant before the tongue hits, then plants, Louie down on his hands and with his white—I'm up, poised, Dedra ain't registered a thing—bare knees and body skidding along the sidewalk like a roach with Dedra's barely-resumed, slow swing, the boy's back arching, tongue sliding up the back of the sweat-soaked, deep-black thigh, rising up to the half-moon of her ass I know's got to be poking out of those cutoffs, Dedra hitching again, Louie's tongue pausing and perhaps holding there on the ass and the little boy's body lurching, exploding forward to keep up.

I take off in a sprint her way just as she finally seems to register the sensation of baby-man tongue on her butt. The palm of her right hand comes barreling round and catches little Louie hard on his left cheek. She takes a step. He falls forward onto the concrete, panting and smiling.

"GAME on," said Louie.

I popped open my fresh beer and looked coldly up into his face, his pockmarked cheeks, the shaggy beard, curly red hair that might not have been combed a day in its life. The board was set—Louie black, J. Red.

"All that time you had her like this," Louie describing hooks with each of his index fingers, fitting them together, pulling. "Had her all tied up and you let her get away." He went on about how like a layabout it was of me to let the house go all to pot after she'd moved in, me spending nights foreman on third shift when God knew I wouldn't be taking but a 5 percent pay cut for a switch to a first-shift line job. "Goddamn knows," he said, "when you had that fine lady all more or less locked up in there just waiting for you to come round to please ! Yes ! please her! And you know that's where you screwed up, the point of it all, goddamnit!" He banged the edge of the table with a closed fist—checkers went flying.

"Now see what you done," I said. A cheap shot, here. I waved my hand, palm up, over the table, was quick to remind him of his own old failures, the old rangy hag Bess he married after he dropped out of high school.

"Better than nothing," he said, went on staring at the space above my head like a dead man. Another cheap shot, cheat. I drank. Then: "Your wife is a no-good hick," I said. "A fool if there ever was. A drunk at that."

"Well," Louie said, draping his thick arms wide to indicate the table, the beer, me, himself.

"Screw it," I said.

Jo plopped down the plates just in time to defuse the bomb, and we ate, checkerboard shoved over into the empty space against the wall.

WE don't talk about what happened next, and if we do it's always the why, never the what or how or when, because, Louie will say, I came running, flying up the walk with the gleam in my eye of the madman he claims I would later become.

The little boy rose to his feet before I could get to him, running off across the street and up the other side, that early puberty putting a quickness in his feet that was outstripping even my own. Dedra's eyes go wide as I hurl past her, the black cave of her open mouth nothing but a thick trail in my periphery, the sound of whatever she yells garbled, descending in pitch as I pass, yelling out to my boys Dinty and Wes, who I know are out back of Dinty's smoking on a reefer I'd gotten them earlier. Louie's headed for the back of Mama Theresa's, for tiny tunnels through the vines and bushes—tunnels me and Dinty and Wes created ourselves oh so long ago, tunnels we couldn't fit through no more. I'm yelling this to the boys, crossing the street to see lanky six-and-a-half-foot Dinty, eyes wide and stoned crazy, pumping arms and legs around the far side of his house. My own feet churn the sidewalk, the road as I cross it, behind Dinty, whose strides are near twice mine, and Louie don't even get so far as Theresa's front yard before Dinty rails up the walk a pinwheel of fists and knees and catches the white boy in a dive, an expert roll, Louie balanced for an instant on Dinty's massive hand, mid-roll, like he was no more than a grapefruit in the man's palm.

Dinty rolls clean, stops, and sets the boy flat on his back, smile still spread slow and buttery across his burned white face. Dinty glares down. Me and Wes shuffle up on either side of him. "What the hell do you think you're doing?" I say, really pissed at the boy, then, though later who could be mad? He knew what he wanted and went after it.

Why? I would ask him, some other time, not now.

You know exactly why.

We beat hell out of him, even if we couldn't beat the smile. I realized later it was this that lost her, this savage act. She came running up the street as we started in on him, and she didn't say a word as she watched. But there was this lost look in her eyes, the first time I'd ever seen it.

A goddamn tasty woman, that Dedra. You oughta know, Louie would say.

After all the insult and threats of firing, we almost up and quit the bleachery two days ago. "This is no kind of job for a man," I said.

"You telling me," said Louie.

"Are we men?" I said.

Louie just nodded.

AFTER the house went to shit and slumped slowly away from itself like a scared dog, and I'd lost my car, even though here I was foreman, just before Louie quit school and came to work at 16 under me at the bleachery, long after it'd become standard protocol for you to find me on the streetcorner talking to myself just as soon as at home or work, after I'd come home one day after weeks and weeks of Dedra's lost eyes and a solid drunk and the woman just wasn't there—I came to know what lost her. The start of it, anyway.

We left little Louie blistered and bleeding puffy-face-up in the hot sun out front of Theresa's. Thought we'd killed him when, an hour later, we came back by and he was still lying there, blood seeping from the left corner of his mouth and pooling in a slight dark circle on the pavement. Like he died there with a smile on his face.

I might have been looking at a ghost, though Louie's got lives like a cat. "How's that fish?" I asked.

"Same as always," he said, then forking a good-size chunk and popping it into his mouth.

"Damn good," I said, smiled.

We ate slow, one strip at a time, but soon enough it'd be gone and I'd look at my watch.

"Hey Jo! How bout a coupla more beers!"

We'd head out only after I'd whipped him for once, the very last game we'd play. We stood out front of the textile mill slack-shouldered on the sidewalk. "Ever thought about working here?" Louie said.

I envisioned that rangy hag of a wife he's got in there with a rag tied tight around her head, sweating over some machine.

"Nope," I said. "You?"

"I wonder what it's like," Louie said. "Bess worked here, but she never talked about it."

It just seemed right. "I guess we should get back," I said.

And we walked back to Jo's for another beer a-piece, standing at the counter jawing with the proprietor about how his liquor license was turning us into a couple no-good paupers. The man pulled on his pointy beard the entire time. That wonderful man.

When we ambled up to the bleachery the parking lot gates were locked. We were an hour late and the third lunch shift was on its way out. I recognized boys who worked under me, tried calling out their names, then laughed when they didn't respond. I tried to get others to let us in, laughed when they guardedly swung the gate closed in our faces. "I think this is it, J.," Louie said, pointing across the parking lot to the building. Here come Oglethorpe.

"You boys goddamn well should've been back by now," he said.

I looked to Louie. He said: "If you're gonna fire us, why don't you just go on."

He went on.

I yelled out for Annie a couple times. Didn't help. Oglethorpe flung his hand up over his head at us to be gone.

Well worth it, though—we each got the other of that bastard's patent-leather wingtips with a gummy spit wad through the gate before it was all over.

"Any idea where Dedra might be these days?" Louie said.

"Goddamnit, you ain't gonna cry again."

"No," he said. "Any idea?"

"Got a vague one," I said.

We jumped in my slightly newer T-Bird—compared to the last, anyway—and hit I-77 to Charlotte doing 90 mph before we left the onramp. We got arrested. Drunk and disorderly, screaming for the woman up into the glass and steel of the sky-scrapers at Tryon.

We were out of the cell by nightfall, because even a couple jackasses like us have friends, if not jobs. We called Louie's buddy, old boy Albert Ledbetter, and he called in a favor. He has no job, either, but somehow he gets on. Give it time, Ledbetter said, because the shit works itself out, your existing. That or somebody gets mad at you and kills you.

Well worth it—that last game.

"GAME on," said Louie.

The board was go, set, ready…

"One more," said Louie. "Screw Oglethorpe, Scrooge bastard." We were fifteen minutes beyond our restart at that point. Five minutes and Louie already had three kings on his plate. Someone told me always answer a cheat with a cheat. "Louie, there's something I never got out of you," I said.

"What's that?"

"I think you well know." His concentration honed, lighted on a jump. He made it. I was down to four reds against his double number of blacks, three of them kings.

"Nossir, I don't," he said.

"What she tasted like, man, that day…"

Louie flinched, eyes filled with haze, lips curling half to a smile. I filched one of his kings from the board, slipping it into a pants pocket.

"You need another beer?" I said.

He didn't answer. I made my jump. "Your turn," I said, flicking the casualty down the length of the table. It rattled against the walls. "Jo! Get this man a beer here!"

"Goddamnit, I think you should know," Louie said.

"Know what?"

"That taste?" Louie stared into the ceiling, then downing the last of the can in front of him.

"Mmm…" I flicked another of the kings from the table. Jo came over with the beer. "Check this," I said to him, pointing down at the table.

"You red?" Jo asked.

"Of course. Black usually wins, but red might just take it today."

"Good luck," Jo said, turning back to the register.

Louie looked down at the beer, at the board. "You been cheating," he said, flat.

"So tell me, Mr. Murphy, tell me."

"You should know."

"I don't, can't remember." My confession of the day. Louie looked me in the eye for the first in a long, long time. His eyes are a deep brown, like mine. Then his head fell back like a limp dick. I said, "Feeling sick lately. Sick like I wake up aching, can't remember who told me to get up. Or if maybe I told myself and forgot it."

"She tasted—" Louie's head still back, eyes closed.

"Yeah?" I said, pulling the last of his kings from the board and sliding it into my front shirt pocket.

"She tasted—" and now his head pulled slowly upward, level, those deep brown eyes odd against the bright white of his face, the red hair. "She tasted incandescent."

"Like a light bulb?"

"Yeah, incandescent, like a light bulb."

"Christ, man, are you gonna cry or what? Jo! Get me another beer!" I jumped the last of all his blacks with a single red, legitimately. He didn't even notice. "Checkmate," I said. "Nice game."

"Checkmate is chess, man," he said, and I shot my hand out for a shake. He glanced at it, but didn't take it.

grandpa's brag book.

"PAW Paw's got a rabbit and three legs on us and he's been holding the bunny for two months!" My brother Glen was hot on his weekly phone call to Charlotte. "You gotta get out here and take it back, man."

I reminded him that I wasn't a regular player. When I hit the links over the border in South Carolina with them—Glen; my pop, Ron; his crazy friend Chip Stricker the used-car salesman; and of course Paw Paw—if I actually came off the 18th green with the rabbit, the old men would force me to free it for their next round. Normally ownership of the rabbit transferred indefinitely. The rabbit—physically it's this beat-up Bugs Bunny head cover meant to go on a particular day's winner's driver, biggest club in the bag, but it's more an idea, something to keep the round interesting, to hold over the head of your opponent like a freshly killed deer, a trophy. You had to win a hole square to get the rabbit, someone else had to win one to free it. If you held the rabbit and won another hole before anyone freed it, you got a leg. What my brother was telling me that fateful day was that my grandfather, the 75-year-old Vincent Jones, whom we called Paw Paw, with a rabbit and three legs was four holes ahead of the pack and "I can't stand it when he's got the bunny," my brother went on. "You know how he is, gloating over you that he's so damn old you oughta be giving him baths, or acting so senile he forgets that he's winning and that's even worse, cause you well know he's faking it. Plus the stupid expression on the rabbit's face is all cartoon laughing at you. It's humiliating."

Paw Paw did hold at least a slight competitive advantage over my father and young Glen and even Stricker, considering the old man had been a club pro up until a few years ago—even made a stab at the tour in his younger days—but it was also partly true that they should have been able to beat him at least occasionally. It was the psychology of his game that put him over the top. The wizened old crow had a keen eye for your weakest parts.

Glen was so insistent I told him I'd do my best to be out there Saturday morning, but I wasn't promising anything. It was Labor Day weekend, and Friday there was a party my wife was forcing me to go to at the house of a bunch of idiot Charlotte bankers who thought we were something special, "artistic types"—I worked for the newspaper, my wife was a retail clerk at a clothing boutique. Pop and my brother and that crazy Stricker were the first off the tee on Saturdays at their golf club, Labor Day weekend or not. I'd have to watch the booze, make it an early morning.

But we hit the party and my wife accused me of playing aloof with the idiot bankers, though my biggest offense happened to be humming the tune to *Rawhide* while one of the fools went on about buying the work of some half-assed Charlotte sculptor who used discarded plastic cups from college keg parties as his raw material. I got depressed, and hence drank more than my fair share of the host's handle of Maker's Mark—the next morning my head throbbed when I pulled into the Tuckaway Ridge parking lot to find Paw Paw sitting on the tailgate of his old F150, grinning, a Polaroid camera in his hand and that filthy bunny-rabbit head cover on the driver in his bag next to him. "Morning, honey," he said. "You look like shit. Glen call you down to beat me, I take it."

It wasn't the first time, of course, and as I've intimated the old man wasn't half as senile as he let on. He laughed a little and handed me a small book—"Grandpa's Brag Book" was emblazoned in white across its front against a garish background of tiny clip-art pictures of tricycles and old-timey roller skates and other things.

"You gave me this for Christmas a long time ago," Paw Paw said. "Used to have pictures of you grandkids in there, but I found a better use for it. My latest is in the rear." I was a little embarrassed that he associated the cheap thing with me. Inside were cardboard double-paned pages with spaces for pictures, presumably yes, of grandkids, but Paw Paw had inserted shots of himself next to his golf bag, the cartoon Bugs face shining atop it. Under each was a date, marking, I assumed, his winnings. "Your brother loves it," Paw Paw said, and I tried to laugh but could only manage an unconvincing half-guffaw. Clearly the old man had too much time on his hands, which is really what I thought of the entire rabbit enterprise, not just his part in it. The rest of the men were "duffers," common terminology for the weekend golfer who comes out and hacks it around like a Neanderthal week after week after week, never advancing an inch in his game. But I guess that wouldn't explain the former club pro's relish.

Fact was, I could beat the old geezer. I benefited from a lack of time around him, thus little opportunity for him to get his wily prods into the solid mental core wherein lies the focus to excel at the game. Clearly, Paw Paw's brag book was him starting early. I'd do best to walk away quickly.

Golf is a game of routine. The professionals, like Paw Paw, learn to make access to the routine and the concurrent mental focus comparably easy, near automatic. The weekend duffer—my father, brother, Stricker and maybe even me—had to play regularly to advance any kind of score. That or you cheat, place all your hopeful luck on the potential success of booze, my own personal trick. Booze calms the mind, eases the body into its rhythm, for the duffer's memory fades quickly as frustration mounts over the course of the day.

I told Paw Paw that, yes, Glen had called me down to beat him, and he could look forward to a fierce competition.

"What do you think of that book?" he said. "Pretty nice?"

And I laughed genuinely, handing it back and setting off alone for the clubhouse, head pounding, to load up on beer. When Glen and my Pop arrived, they found me drinking my second tallboy in the driver's seat of a golf cart I'd claimed for the round. Paw Paw was on his way to my cart before I quickly motioned Glen to join me. "I gotta stay away from him," I said. "Took you guys long enough."

My headache was melting away with the hangover. Pop took the seat next to Paw Paw, who didn't say a word as we eased the vehicles down to the first tee. "Pop's always been partisan," my brother muttered. I downed the beer and cracked a new one. The boy hit me with the evil eye. "You know it's 7 a.m., don't you?" he said. "Better watch it. I need you today, son of a bitch."

I pulled my tee shot into a sand trap on the left side of the fairway and, like all of us but Paw Paw, double-bogied the hole. Paw Paw'd gained a fourth leg on the rabbit—hell of a bad way to start. I popped my fourth beer, and Glen laid into me about it a little. I told him my secret. The more drunk you are the less you think.

"Huh," he said. "Well shit, give me one of those."

On the second hole, Stricker smashed a drive right down the middle, aced the approach shot and parred the hole, Paw Paw saving a bogey himself, amazingly, after losing a ball to the woods. Stricker advanced all of us one leg on the rabbit chase. Stricker was between my and my father's age, close to 40. He had a couple kids, though, and so acted around me and my brother like a grandfather, which put him occasionally in Paw Paw's camp. He was constantly inventing excuses for his usually godawful play—today it was his back, which he'd suggested before the first hole he'd thrown out while in bed with a highly unfortunate young woman. "I thought your back was bothering you," I said, after his magnificent performance on No. 2.

He removed his mirrored sunglasses and gloated a little. "A little cheese for your whine, son." Which wasn't funny in the least, and a joke he used every goddamn chance he got. My brother let it go, congratulating him in his way on taking back one of the legs from Paw Paw for us all. "That'll show the old coot," Glen spat at Stricker.

In the chase for the rabbit, the leader was everyone's enemy. One challenger's small victory fed directly into the camps of the other players. I stood stony-eyed, with yet another double bogey, the weekend duffer's most humiliatingly accessible memory. I opened the last of the six beers I had and finished it by the end of the third hole, which I parred. "All right, game on, goddamnit," I muttered. I was dizzy with drink; it wasn't even eight o'clock yet.

HALF done, at the end of the first nine, my body was screaming for more booze, but I'd settled into a groove in my game, just so, and Paw Paw and his brag book were fading. Between me and crazy Stricker, who'd brought along his trombone to toot should the bunny be set free, we'd taken back the rabbit's three legs and the old Bugs Bunny head cover hung to Paw Paw's driver by a thread, screaming, cackling to be released. I picked up another sixer at the turn, my brother joining in with a pint of Jim Beam, convinced of the elixir's power. And from the 10th hole's tee box, I looked over at the kid's expectant eyes and Stricker positively beaming and I was drunk, yes, but on, goddamnit, after a birdie tie with Paw Paw on number nine and he hadn't said a thing since—which looking back on it might should have been ominous, I guess—and my normally ornery

Pop was near to invisible, having a hell of a bad day and sitting smug and silent in the golf cart with the old man. I thought of my wife and her idiotic anger and the stupid bankers and teed off with a three iron to lay up just to the edge of the water hazard on this par four, a short dog-leg left with the hazard just at the fairway's turn, and damned if I didn't hit it dead solid perfect. The memory accessed on such a shot is below the level of the cerebrum, all in the bones and muscle and, when you hit it and you barely even feel it—though the club head moves at however many hundreds of miles per hour and the ball is just sitting there solid, resolute, before it goes sailing through the air a physical miracle, silent as a snowy winter night—it's a moment of indescribable beauty. My brother let fly a loud "whoo!" as I pulled the club down from my follow-through. He began a round of hand claps, and Stricker didn't gloat but rather gave a ceremonial bow.

"Goddamn son," he said. "That gives me a good feeling. One hell of a lay-up."

The ball sat right where I wanted it, just before the water with a simple five-iron shot remaining to the green. But Paw Paw was up next, and the ancient man was holding his driver.

"You ain't gonna try to clear that water," Stricker said.

"That's suicide for a man your age," I said, and I laughed and shook my head in disbelief, for that was exactly what he was about to do. He teed the ball up, stood back to gaze down the length of the fairway and, without even a practice swing, let her rip.

The ball sailed long away past my shot over the trees and water and I'd never before seen anyone do anything like that, much less this 75-year-old. He really let the gloating begin. "Now that's something to be proud of, honey," the old man said.

"Goddamnit!" my brother spat, pulling on the bottle of bourbon under Pop's mildly disapproving gaze. Paw Paw was turning his game up, but when we got to the green, after a beauty of a second shot that I left two feet from the hole, Paw Paw had only a par. I sunk my putt for birdie. And with that, the rabbit had been set free.

It was a solemn moment. Paw Paw, his head down but with a grin stuck to his face all the while, took the ragged Bugs Bunny head cover from his bag and handed it to my father, always the ceremonial leader, if he rarely actually led, whose voice then boomed through the trees at the back of the hole: "The— Rabbit—Has—Been—Freed!"

Stricker played a version of taps on his trombone and we all bowed our heads for the next thing. Pop continued, "Let—the—Golden—Chase—Commence!" which I never understood, really, though these folks were way into the theater of it all, at least my brother and father were. Stricker always appeared a bit bemused behind his Ray-bans and the mouthpiece of the trombone, but you could never tell with him.

And now, with the rabbit free, we were in it for keeps. There were birdies going down on every hole. With the field even, the pressure was off. Muscle memory set into the bodies of the weekend warriors, including Paw Paw, who now birdied near every hole, it seemed, though one of us invariably came through to tie him, to keep the rabbit free. It came down to the last, and my brother, you see, he was determined that it remain free or at least I win it just to let it go again. He was a mighty drunk by now, too, so that magnified the stakes. As we bounced down to the low-set 18th tee, he was cursing and putting the pressure on. "Why don't *you* go for the win," I kept saying, but he still wouldn't shut up.

"It's up to you, man!" he kept on. "I'm messed-up, man, I can't win! Dontchoo let him win!"

The final hole was a challenge, sure—it favored a long ball striker—a short porch par five with a strong uphill grade. And though I was 40 years the junior of the old man, he could still belt it farther. And he did. His second shot left him with a short chip for eagle. I was looking at a 30-foot birdie putt. My brother was scowling. "Don't let him put you away," he said. He sulked like a mad baby. "I don't know what I'll do if he walks away from here with that bunny!"

"Glen, it really ain't that big a deal," I said. He looked crazy, eyes bloodshot with the bourbon, which he'd finished back on number 16. And then he looked for his salvation elsewhere. "Stricker, whatchoo layin'?" But we all knew Stricker was putting for par, as was everybody but me and Paw Paw. It appeared only I could save us. Paw Paw chipped onto the green and put the ball a few feet from the hole, a veritable gimme for birdie. I had to make a 30-foot putt to keep the rabbit running.

After the old man tapped in, I lined up my putt, stood over the ball and took a deep breath, a little woozy now from all the drink and the sun and the heat, out here, Labor Day weekend in Carolina. I closed my eyes and let the rhythm of the putt take over. When I opened them, the ball was sailing by an inch to the right of the hole, turning slowly, slowly but not enough.

"Goddamnit!" Glen spat, throwing his putter from the green out across the cart path to the lawn before the clubhouse, where it landed and sprung end over end over end. "Keep your damn temper in check, boys," Pop finally weighing in on the pettiness of it all. "My God. You shouldn't be drinking this much, either."

"The Lord don't like a drunkard, it's true," Stricker chimed in, adjusting his Ray-Bans.

The old guys then putt out, finishing the round. Paw Paw approached me with his hand outstretched. "Good round, honey," he said. "Mind taking a picture for me?" And we moved over to his cart, where my father was rooting around for the head cover. As we approached, he looked back at us all wide-eyed and said, "It's gone!"

Then Paw Paw, who went for his brag book, realized it too was gone. We could see the culprit, now, my drunk brother, facing us across the cartway on the empty driving-range tees. "See if you can catch me, duffers!" he yelled, holding up the Bugs head cover and Paw Paw's little book, then went running off into the woods at the edge of the clearing. We all just stared.

"Well," I said.

"You really should lay off the drink," Pop said, "particularly around him."

"All right," I said.

"You give me a ride home?" he said. "Your brother's got the keys to my car."

"Sure," I said. "You drive." And Paw Paw, sitting in his cart set to drive off in pursuit of what was rightly his, wished me better luck next time, laughing, gunning the little electric motor, and I yelled that he could fuck off and me and my pop drove on home. We talked about the fight I had with my wife, and he said I might do well to get her some flowers.

"But I am in the right," I said. He gave me a sarcastically withering look. "All right," I said. We stopped at a florist. With that deed done, we spent the rest of the way as all duffers, losers, do. We talked about the game.

death in Hammond.

MY buddy Mort got married on April Fool's Day, 2005, his reasoning at upwards of 40 years old somewhere between a practical wager and blissful capitulation—both on or to the woman, if you ask me, though I'm not too young to be aware of the two-way street of these things.

Before all that, there was a bachelor party, of course, and even before that I had him over in lieu of a formal celebration for our yearly get-drunk over the Daytona 500 to start the year out right.

My relationship to NASCAR is a mite complicated, as is any Southern expat's, but it essentially fits the following parameters:
1) I don't typically much care for its fans, unless they're related to me—Mort's an exception.
2) I was raised on a steady diet of Richard Petty and Dale Earnhardt, but when Earnhardt died I was a long way from Calvary Baptist in Charlotte, N.C., and I was mostly amused by the news of the regional, may have even been national, TV coverage his service received (delivered via a fitful, sobbing telephone call from my redneck brother).
3) Chili goes well with it.
4) Beer too.

Mid-February and the first race of the season, the grand Daytona 500, came on quick this year, but I met it in plenty of time to muster my few friends for the end-of-Speed Week hangout at my place: plenty of chili, plenty of beer, and in addition to Mort there was Erk, a nonfan, as it goes, but a man with a large beard who shared a name with the famed Georgia Southern football coach (formerly of the UGA junkyard dawgs defense) Erk Russell. Erk's likewise a man with a mind open to pretty much anything, really, and particularly the idea that a latent homosexuality pervades much of men's professional sports and its enthusiasts, an idea very hard to discount at any moment—Erk makes a hell of an argument.

And Henry David Cocteau, whom we call HD, also a nonfan but from North Carolina, which makes us brothers, of a sort, in Chicago. HD's attraction to NASCAR is all regional nostalgia, boyhood memories of sitting with Pop by the wood fireplace talking Earnhardt bump-steer and old Richard Petty lore.

And Mort, of course, a new-NASCAR enthusiast if I've ever seen one—he wears an earring with his DeWalt cap and diminutive wrap-around shades. His enthusiasm for Matt Kenseth seems to spring from an apparently loyalty to DeWalt tools, not that he ever uses them, really; he does live in Chicago, city of big service, and works in a bar far (metaphysically, if not geographically) from any real garage.

We were primed. Or at least I was. My brother, however, was ecstatic. He lives for this shit. Good ol' boy Dale Jarrett, among the old guard of drivers in our time, had won the shootout pole position-determining race the previous week and thus my brother put all the money he could afford on the man in one of those offshore online-gambling ops. He'd been calling me daily over the preceding week with news from South Carolina, from the heart of the near-psychotic fandom that resides somewhere in his left brain. He "couldn't fucking wait" for the green flag, when Jarrett would by any means necessary whip every other driver out there. Yes, to hear the boy talk you'd have thought he was a shoe-in for victory.

When race time arrived, chili beginning its fourth and final hour of simmering, beer on the back porch cooling naturally in the Chicago winter, after a viewing of the unfortunate singing of none other than former beauty queen and *Playboy* pinup Vanessa Williams and countless country losers, me and Mort—HD and Erk hadn't yet arrived—watched Jarrett promptly lose 20 spots due to a quickly failing tire. My brother called and was cursing, over the phone. Mort invoked the great Dale Earnhardt when I passed him the handheld, brother in mid-curse, as he said, "That's racin'."

I listened to the attendant yowling, Mort painfully pulling the receiver away from his ear, with equal parts glee and empathetic consternation, for the NASCAR fan is like his favorite driver and competitive to a fault, though likewise always mindful of the ever-present possibility of death. My brother and I are inveterate hypochondriacs. In fact, I was on the front end of one of my months-long attacks for the 500 this year, and as Mort put the phone on the floor, where my cat had proceeded to sniff at it, then screeching a little at my brother's voice blasting forth, I turned my head again to the television just in time for a spectacular wreck involving three of the tour's no-names, sending a spike of pain through my lower left ribcage, whereupon my mind seized on the pain and my heart beat loudly in my chest. I lit a cigarette. "Damn," Mort said, pointing stupidly to the TV, then to the phone on the floor, from which my brother's voice now could be heard saying "Hey! You there? Was that a damn cat?" He hung up, eventually, and wouldn't call back again, not even when Jarrett was charging through the field toward the front at the end of the race, when it looked like Jarrett might actually contend for this one. It was a shame, too, cause had he called to gloat it would've blown up square in his face just like Jarrett's chances for victory: I try never to lose an opportunity to get one up on my brother, and in being a racing fan it was too easy. The highly partisan fan suffers with his driver. I was relatively nonpartisan, if occasionally I pulled (along with the rest of my small crew here except for Erk, who couldn't give a shit either way) for Mark Martin, at the time another old-guard veteran we couldn't help but be partial to on account of the grand tragedy of his corporate sponsor, the erectile dysfunction drug Viagra. It's not something we'll even much talk about, you know, until Martin creeps into the top five, maybe, or say it's getting late in the race and the little ticker across the top of your TV might be telling you, lap by lap, that the old man's creeping up toward the front and then, with maybe 50 laps left in whatever race, you might feel compelled to put all shame aside and raise a toast to the victims of erectile dysfunction the world over, to raise one for the blue No. 6 Viagra Ford of Mark Martin, native of Batesville, Ark.

Yes, the old boy Dale Jarrett finished 15th after reaching the top ten and I imagined my brother was none too pleased (goodbye, $500). But Martin, well, let's just say that me and HD and Mort spent the last 20 laps of that year's Speed Week silent as elves, our eyes and minds locked on the events at hand. Martin was shifted back and forth between second and third and fourth places in the final laps, before a wreck back in the field and ensuing caution period, after which the youthful power trio of Dale Earnhardt Jr., Jeff Gordon, and defending season champion Kurt Busch fought it out to a Gordon victory. The driver of the Viagra car finished sixth in what was purported at the time to be his last-ever Daytona 500 (he reneged on his retirement plans later in the year, though), but it wasn't such a bad showing. Me and Mort and HD were all down, a little, though the drinks probably had something to do with it.

But Erk was beaming, always a joke at arm's length, if not in hand. "Martin blew his load, didn't he? Or maybe he just couldn't get it up," Erk said. We scowled, went out back for the cold that clears the air, for a cigarette, another beer. Take the day onward, we figured in our sudden dysfunctional camaraderie. Young and defeated all. On to the Rainbo bar, where we knew some people, even if we had to take the traitor namesake of the great Georgia football coach. Erk came out onto my porch as we all shivered and lit up our second cigarettes and invited himself along, but it didn't much matter. At the bar, Erk even joined in on a toast to Martin's failure, likewise our own. My shoulder burned, now. I cracked the tension out, poured the shot down my throat and thought, if we ever grew up and got married and started careers and all that, God help us. Mort was on his way, anyway, and I wouldn't remember much after the toast, wouldn't see any of them again before Mort's bachelor party two months later.

The celebration—or collective lament, as bachelor parties go—began at a Chicago Franklin Street steak house known for its asinine attitude toward the plebeians who frequented its halls hoping to brush elbows with the nation's elite. Consequently, the prices were jacked to beyond even reasonable extremes, said elites enjoyed the comfort of the first-floor bar and cushioned booths, and the rest of us, well, we were relegated to a cavernous dining hall upstairs where the volume of conversation from neighboring tables forbade even the possibility of communication rendered in anything under a shout. Thankfully, I had to work through most of this first portion, so I missed out on contributing my $100-plus to the final tab when I got there, Mort and company shortly on their ways to the door and each of the men in his own way—some surreptitiously eyeing, some outright ogling, one to the point of even snapping a few pictures—with his gaze stuck to the dignitary across the room, Mr. Keanu Reeves, aka Neo, aka Ted in *Bill and Ted's Excellent Adventure*, by far his best flick. The picture taker, a character I knew only as the organizer of the evening's festivities, a man close to my age, younger than most in this party of near middle-agers—Mort was 15 years my senior—was collared by the bartender and reprimanded very haughtily. I laughed a little too loudly for the situation's gravity, and the organizer blushed mightily. I chanced a long glance Neo's way on our forced way out the door. Keanu Reeves had to be nearing 40 himself, I figured, though he looked the very picture of 28, my own age. I clutched my chest; the possibility of death, on a night like this, was ever near.

And soon enough we were afloat in Jack Binion's Horsehoe Casino—in Lake Michigan just off the coast of industrial Hammond in northwest Indiana. On each floor of the giant boat, way off in a corner but close enough to the floor-to-floor stairwells to be quite conspicuous to the more than casual observer, placards hung on the walls with directives as to the appropriate course of action in the event of the boat's capsizing. At first I thought they had to be a sardonic joke on the part of the owners. Clearly the quadruple-decker casino was in no conventional sense a boat. We were not sailing or, I suspected, even floating. Mort filled me in, though, on the machinations of the last decade or so of Midwest casino law, in particular that of Illinois and Indiana, the latter of whom beat the former to the punch by allowing casinos to open at all, in the early 1990s, following a decision by the state of Iowa, in turn, in the late '80s to allow gambling during sailing excursions, the rationale being that if casinos were relegated to the state's waterways, any attendant social disruption in the surrounding communities would be avoided.

The Iowa and subsequent Indiana casino-gaming industries, as Mort called them, believe it or not, hoping as they did to encourage tourism, thus struggled from the beginning—the inconvenience of waiting to sail and then return produced a dearth of idle tourist-gamblers, encouraging only the professionals, who were wily and prone to winning, of course. The take of the operator, the state, was incorrigibly low.

Then Illinois, sandwiched between the two states and within striking distance of residents of each, introduced its own version of riverboat gambling but quickly went dockside, on example of the Mississippi model, allowing for permanent air-conditioned gangways, free 24-hour access to and from gaming parlors, and popular participation, generally, the drawing in of suckers from all over the region and beyond. This killed Indiana's enterprise, until they followed with exactly the same thing. Hence the relative absurdity of life-preserver directions, one had to think.

Or maybe not.

Mort couldn't relieve my mind of the logistical, physical question that remained about the boat's "docked" status—were we floating on water, or were we somehow moored by a solid superstructure under the boat's base, immune to any possible rising or falling water level and from the rocking attendant to the arrival of any tsunami- or otherwise smaller-size wave?

"It's a boat, man," Mort said. "Boats float."

Mort is a lover of life—temperless, loud and boisterous. I wish he and the wife well. As for me, I wasn't convinced; death was on the mind. Still coming out of the bout of hypochondria that began more than a month before, I remained half-convinced I had lung and throat cancers (as I continued to chain-smoke), diabetes, and astronomically high blood pressure at once and that my heart would give out at any moment. I was walking around, smoking, drinking, breathing. It's a weakness of mine: the existentence of death, the very fact that it ever happened, was enough to lead me to this kind of thinking.

Plus, after every beer consumed, on the walk to the bar in the high-stakes parlor on the third level, my chest pounded harder at every imagined keen of the floor, the absolutely level whiskey glass atop Mort's chosen slot machine be damned. The ship was sinking, I convinced myself. "Do you feel that?" I said after my fifth trip to the bar. Mort, self-described "slot junkie," was engaged now with a contraption that had a winning hit matrix extended beyond just a single line across the slot screens to include a myriad other possible combinations along a grid that took up a majority of the display.

"Feel what?" Mort said. He hit the maximum bet button, in this case equal to a ten-dollar wager, and the wheels rolled, stopping with a series of BARs spread diagonally across the display grid. The machine bleeped happily but put Mort up only two dollars. The improved odds on this particular style of machine seemed to feed or enhance the addictive properties of the compulsive behavior. Mort lost a hundred dollars on this one alone, but it took him damn near two hours to do it. The apotheosis of the law of diminishing returns, the slots will hit on a maximum bet occasionally, and you'll still be down two bucks, depending on the corners of the grid you match. Only rarely do you score a direct hit. Then, it'll let you win a buck or two back, then go down only four after betting ten. It's a bullshit game, and this I told Mort.

"I've won big before," he grinned up at me. Of course. This is the problem. As in life and death, anything's possible, you tell yourself, and maybe even rightly so. You know your own history, anyway, that time you went up $200 on a single-line slot and cashed out, called it a night.

Mort went up overall tonight after a big hit on another machine, and I was like, "You oughta give it up right there, man." But Mort only grinned, sarcastically, under his handlebar mustache. He took his ticket on to the next machine. "If I quit now, I'm only up fifteen bucks for the night," he said. "Shit, I've done better than that."

Anything's possible. HD, who like me was here only on behalf of Mort and consequently only interested in the drinks at the bar, got married at one of the lored drive-through chapels in Las Vegas. An auto aficionado, you might call him, he and his gal went on a long road trip in the '61 Chrysler he'd kept up since the mid-'80s in Florida, in the '90s hauling it to Chicago, where it now spends the winters in a garage and still gets along quite well, or so HD says. The romantic all-possibilities sense behind the trip took its toll, as he explains it—plus they'd bandied the idea of a Las Vegas wedding about in the weeks preceding the excursion—so with the juggernaut they rode approaching the desert casino city and the ease of obtaining a marriage license ($55 and a valid ID, he said) high in their minds, they jumped.

Las Vegas is of course the envy of all locales that would bolster the city government's coffers by offering big-box casino gaming; their cheap marriage licenses are part of the tourist economy, too, as are requirements written into the local code that hotels with a certain high number of rooms come with a particular square footage of casino space. Indiana's nowhere near there; looking around I could recognize more than a few faces from the city and a number of men and women who, to my stereotyping gaze, had that hangdog tired look one gets from working at a steel mill all day (Gary Works, not to mention a number of other large factories, was 15 minutes down the road), and in general the air is full of local desperation. Indiana doesn't require the existence of large hotels along with their riverboats, as does for instance Mississippi, where Biloxi and Tunica county south of Memphis had long since become destinations to rival Atlantic City. And Hammond, along with much of the industrial northern Indiana shores, with the collapse of the American industrial economy complete, was a veritable bastion of macroeconomic decay. It seemed obvious to me that the casino could only serve the purpose of completing the death, sucking the region's desperate denizens dry. Naturally, though I lived among the bright lights of the ivory tower to the north, this includes me.

The more disgustingly drunk I got, the less hope I had.

By the end, I would pull a hundred from my bank account and wade through the slots, emulating Mort's method of picking the lucky machine, whereby he waves his right arm in front of each until one makes a sound he deems worthy of a winner. My technique was decidedly less lucky, or less developed, if you prefer, as it took me a mere 20 minutes to wipe out my hundred. I found HD by a blackjack table with the remainder of our party, sans the bachelor still wading through slots on the floor above us. Here, essentially below-decks, minus the continual bleeping of the slots, one could listen carefully and almost hear the telltale creak of the floating or sinking casino, or one could well imagine it, as did I as HD watched the folks at the blackjack table engaged in a to-the-death round. It was quickly becoming clear that the party's organizer was something of a gambling junky. He was losing big-time but was all wide-eyed glee. The only female with us—a lesbian who in a bit of fence-hopping HD at least couldn't approve of (in fact, he was vocal about his disapproval, shaking a fist into the air and bemoaning the fact that she) would be attending the bachelorette party as well ("Boundaries!" boomed HD, "boundaries, dude. They exist for reasons." I tipped back my last beer and laughed heartily.)—was pulling in gobs of cash. And as we stood there, waiting, Mort walked up alone and shot his thumb to the door, he wanted to make last call at his favorite bar back in the city. But these folks were high on the lesbian's winnings, or on the organizer's losses, or both. I smoked a cigarette and closed my eyes. "This motherfucker's floating," I said, as I imagined I could feel the ground swaying, buoying me up, then dropping me down, with it. "I can feel it," I said. I let my head roll way back.

Before I passed out, it was Mort's voice in ear, cutting through the clamor of voices at the blackjack table. "It ain't Fool's Day yet," it said. "Shut the fuck up."

does anybody really know what time it is?

I was walking down the street one day. My watch broke a couple weeks before on a flight from California.

The clocks in downtown Birmingham, sweet home Alabama, where I roamed, read various times and temperatures. Above a bank a digital reading said 3 a.m., Monday morning. It was sunny, it was hot. It was Sunday. An old clockface on a 1st Avenue building was stopped at noon. Or midnight. Had to be near 2:30 or something.

I met a friend at the bar and we sweated and had a few drinks. He wasn't wearing a watch and his wife had left him.

Middle of damn sob story: bad moment to bring up the time.

I wanted to talk about the generals, anyway, who were saying "this Iraq shit is fucked" in the papers all week—that was the gist of it, at least. My friend wasn't having it. People like to talk about their personal problems. Nobody likes to talk about generals except journalists and gunheads. It's pretty hard to get the journalists going, really. In California, at least, they would go on a little, but everybody would go on a little there. In Birmingham it was tough, as taboo as time.

My friend had escaped before I got a chance to ask. The bar's clock was broken. Not a cell phone in sight. We are virtual Luddites down here, I say.

I walked. Guy in a mid-80s Cadillac offered me a ride on his way out of town to Montgomery. Which sounds like a joke, I know, that might end at a flea market that's just like a mini mall.

I said I wished he'd take me by the old clock tower in English Village in Mountain Brook, among the granola Republicans.

"Is there a clock tower out there?" he said.

"I think so," I said.

The Caddy was beat down, puffing smoke, the minute and hour hands on the busted dash clock poised just left of the 6 position. "Your clock don't work," I said.

"You want to know what time it is, brother?" he said.

Of course I did.

"Just turn around," he said. We were on the 280 interurban, as I often pretentiously called it, by then, headed due southeast. "On the skyscraper, man," he said.

The upper marquee topping the building at Morris and 19th I can't remember the name of. But it was blinking Morse code or something equally incomprehensible.

"It's broke!" I hollered.

The dude got a clear lane ahead and craned his neck around and… "Shit," he muttered. "All right."

It wasn't far to the clock tower anyway, if there was a clock tower, just over the hill, the very next exit, even, around the zoo and the botanical gardens where the granola Republicans all sent their kids to get married.

In the floorboard of the old Caddy was a pair of dusty desert boots. "You in the army?" I said.

He just nodded.

"How do you keep up?" I said.

"I don't know what that means," he said. He nodded slowly to some beat in his brain, I guess. "I keep the time just like any-body else," he said. "Just like your ass." Just out of reach, like me, always behind or ahead, depending on how lucky I might feel on whatever day we're talking about. Today it was less than most, I guess, and I knew then that the truth of this man was less in the boots than in the Krystal burger wrappers clogging the backseat, the discount tobacco he smoked.

"You're not in the army," I said.

"Not the U.S. army," he said. "The people's army. I got that shit right here," and he balled up his right fist and started howl-ing laughter at my wide-eyed surprise. I was a little scared, I'll admit. "S'all right, man," he said. He mashed the brakes at the main corner in the village. "This is your stop. Go on and get out. Have a…" I slammed the door to the Caddy and he pulled away. There was no clock tower in English Village—none that I could see, anyhow—just the Billy bar where the Young Republicans were meeting at that very moment—the sign on the front door said so: WE ARE IN HERE NOW. Signed: YOUNG REPUBLICANS CHAPTER T__. I wanted to talk about the Iraq war. It was Sunday and I figured they might go for it. Don't ask me why. Or when. I don't know what time it was.

have you seen Bella Angeles?

SHE strides through the Chicago night with grins for your frowns and faux outrage at the serendipitous chance of your meeting, in a Taqueria bathroom someplace, it's likely. She had a closet in the men's room at the Gusto, from which she emerged only when the cash flow was low and the messenger was hot. Men, take heed. She'll be watching you through a hole about chest-level above a urinal somewhere in the city: take a shower.

She will venture into your world if you're persuasive. She followed my pal Manny one night to a wedding, acting the very respectable young lady, and then when the tall drinks came out persuading my pal's poor drunk mind into the grass under a banquet table covered with little lady fingers and wine and what all else. They did it behind the cloth on which scrambled remains of the wedding cake sat.

I had it in for her shortly after, which is what I want you to know. Which is what I want her to know—I have the capacity for something other than vengeance. I'm sorry. I loved her.

I could tell you all about her winsome ways, about how she struck out to win me to her side as a method of releasing herself from bondage, but it wouldn't be true. Bella wanted nothing to do with me, mostly. Only once did she allow me to forgo payment—that last time, and by the end of the scuffle in the Gusto's bathroom she was on her way to a night in jail, transaction canceled.

She got me kicked out, you see, banned if not for life then certainly until I took my revenge. Didn't have the patience to suffer me to wait until we got outside someplace before she took it all off, came striding through her little door there as I stood before the urinal still shaking the dew from the end of my thing, I say. You take Gusto away from me and you take my life, I told her, but she just laughed, and I swooned like a little frail from one of the old pulp novels. They couldn't kick her out, she said. If it weren't for her I guess the place might have gone out of business, the burritos in those days were so loose. Illiterates from all around flocked to the place for a piece, it's true. Women, even, to whom the MEN sign on the door meant little, if anything at all. Bella was never so very discriminating that she stayed in the poor house. She made a decent living. But I knew her too well. I knew where she was weak.

I contrived to get into Gusto care of a disguise. I borrowed a dress from my Aunt in Humboldt Park—I told her we had a little dumb show we were working on for a buddy's bachelor party—big blue-and-white polka-dotted thing, I'm sure you've seen them. I puffed up my chest a little with toilet paper and bra, a pitiful and hoary fate for a man, but I buffed myself up all the same in conversation with Manny, as he agreed she'd crossed the line. The object of the contrivance deserved her fate, ruinance, banishment of Bella Angeles.

Bella is deathly afraid of snakes. Her Chicago routine normally took her nowhere near anything remotely resembling one of the hairless ground crawlers, but once we were locked in heat in the back of a pet store on North Avenue, next to what she presumed to be two empty aquariums. I presumed, too, but then the dark insides of one of the fish boxes began to move. Bella's muffled yelps at my thrusts became those of terror as she disengaged, pointing, eyes wide, behind me, where I turned to see the head of a harmless black snake poised above the rim of one of the aquariums, tongue licking the air like it enjoyed our show. She got me kicked out of there, too.

The day of final reckoning I pranced out of a torrential spring rain and into the Gusto with a striped king snake in an old handbag/purse I borrowed (stole, in this case) from the selfsame aunt who'd given me the old dress. The long tails of the thing blew in the draft that sucked into the place as I casually ordered a taco from Eduardo, a man from whom I'd ordered probably 100,000 beers over the years. He blinked a little at my manly made-up face like he couldn't quite believe it neither this early in the day, nor in combination with the dress and bonnet I wore atop my head. Eduardo has seen it all. Maybe, I imagine his mind ran on, the drag clubs up the way were cashing in their newfound cultural capital, hosting their shows in the daylight hours for all to see.

I quietly prodded the snake in my handbag. I kicked the bag, placed as it was against the front wall under my table, and by the time my taco was eaten the old vinyl thing appeared as if it were alive itself, the big bastard inside writhing and squirming so that the bag seemed to breath, bulging in slow rhythm with the life around it. The men behind the counter didn't even bat an eye as I gingerly picked it up and waltzed straight into the MEN's.

"Bella," I called out, putting on a high-priss whine of a voice, heart wildly fluttering all the while.

To no response.

"I've got a gift for you, dear," I said.

Movement behind the wall in front of me. Poised in front of the urinal, I held up the handbag and smiled darkly under my bonnet, held and twirled the handle with thumb and forefinger in presentation. The door to the closet of Ms. Bella Angeles flung wide. There she stood, the exquisite front of her leopard-print dress lit by the bathroom's fluorescent lights against the blackness at her back. Leopard print and leather, boots up to her thighs. "What the fuck, chico," she said. She cased my identity immediately.

I removed the bonnet, moved from the urinal to place myself between her and the door into the greater taqueria. I locked the door.

"What the fuck," she said. I did not speak, could not, my heart in my throat, simply bent low and channeled every ounce of rage I had, stanched the excitement at the sight of her, and zipped open the handbag with a quick flourish. The snake slithered slowly by turns, its red stripes emerging one by one by one until all twelve shown there in maybe ten feet of space between us. "And what do you think?" I said. Her breath came quicker, quicker there in the doorway, Bella paralyzed with fright, I figured, as the snake slithered away from the light, right toward her, passing within inches of her feet and on into the dark. Bella turned slowly as it passed and watched it disappear. "I thought you'd like him," I said. "Come with me. I'll help you."

I looked to where the snake had disappeared when a sharp pain came across my forehead. I guess I blacked out completely, not waking until Eduardo and the rest of the boys behind the counter carried me into the rain, Bella directing traffic just behind them. "Get that motherfucker out of here! Get him out!" She'd hit me over the head with something big, something sharp. Screwing my eyes down—to the tune of some of the most outrageous pain I've felt—I could see blood beginning to coagulate on my lips.

People do not act as you want them to, I know, though I at

least won a slight victory that day. Bella Angeles set up shop some other place. The snake was never found, and the idea that it lurked elsewhere in the place was enough to keep her away. The Gusto was mine.

 # my justice for all.

HAVE you ever been told that you resemble Tom Hanks, the actor?

On my way out the door from my extremely low-paying, phone-pumping job (insurance marketing), soon to be en route to the airport so that I might enjoy time with my outsize New South family in that fat-dumb-and-happy American Thanksgiving time, a coworker passed me in the hallway, turned 180 degrees and latched on to my shoulder. "I've got it!" she said, eyes going wide and happy wrinkles forming in her forehead.

"Oh yeah?" I said.

"You look exactly like Tom Hanks!" she said. "I mean, the resemblance is uncanny. I've been thinking about it for weeks now but couldn't place it."

My boss trundled by on his own way out the door, and, having heard the exchange, nodded in agreement. "She's absolutely correct," he said, shrugging his shoulders as if in confirmation of the dubious quality of the observation.

I nodded dumbly at them. How might one go about responding to such a statement?

You look like Tom Hanks!

Thank you.

No way.

You look like Tom Hanks!

Oh yeah? I'm driving a beat-up old Ford Taurus too! It's true! It's falling apart!

"GEORGE W. Bush is the devil," my younger brother proclaimed. Unmarried at age 30, the man was lucky to be a man in his place of residence, outside Charlotte on the South Carolina side of the border, where we grew up. He hawked industrial chemicals for an outfit on the North Carolina side, frequented strip clubs, and voted Democratic with a vigor uncommon to most men of his kind—read: white—in the area.

He was sweating, he told me on the phone, he was so worked-up angry with paranoia over it. He'd seen the fucking pictures.

He'd seen the pictures?

"He's the devil, man—you can see the goddamn horns on his head," he said. "Look close. They're usually covered by the stupid old-man brush cut he's got, but you can see the lumps, man."

"Well, a lot of people don't like him," I said. "That's no reason to…"

My brother believed lots of things. He once told me Jerry Falwell was a disciple of the church of Satan. I figured aloud that Falwell was little more a simple-minded but charismatic fat idiot with a lot of bad ideas, but brother wouldn't have it: "Jerry Falwell and Anton Levey are known butt lovers," as if that settled it.

Ten years ago, when I first moved to Chicago, it was he who launched the Great Secession of 2641 N. Spaulding, an idea that succeeded for a time in rising above the level of joke at which we normally operated. This was my address, not even a whole building, just a small center block of six apartments and an overloud basement boiler in an otherwise-numbered U-shaped building on the city's northwest side. We had a party, attended by all six of my friends in the town at the time plus one (the apartment couldn't hold much more than that, anyway)—the neighbors weren't invited. But for the heroin addict in one of the third-floor units, I had little knowledge of them.

At the dramatic high point, eight of us standing in the 15-by-15-foot excuse for a living room throwing back canned beers, my brother, bearded, Southern and ugly, drunk as a monk, perched atop my twin bed and raised his fist high. "I declare myself and this apartment and all the people herein the sovereign state of 2641 N. Spaulding!" he hollered. It was unearthly quiet in the little place from then on. I think we watched some *Green Acres* reruns on T.V. and smoked dope.

But what he didn't know was that I'd heard of the horns before—they'd followed me around the country in half-remembered bits of conversation and offhand observations from a host of characters these past few years. Still, coming from him the assertion was news, a new obsession for him, I suspected, that might keep him appropriately raging for at least a year or two more. I rather liked it. Bush had been out of the spotlight so long. Memories flooded in of those purpose-filled years, when the fortunate son did indeed take on a decidedly demonic quality in the heads of the denizens of New Weird America, as the papers were calling the kids in those days. At the same time, I wondered if the hometown church had somehow inspired my brother on the devil count and so made sure to inquire into any recent attendance. "Jesus no I haven't been going! But that don't mean I'm blind," he screamed into the phone. I shuddered, winced, pulled the receiver back from my ear as the train I was on catapulted me through the near south side to the airport. I could just barely hear the next comment, as his voice dropped to a conspiratorial whisper. "Offshore oil drilling," he said. "I've seen it. Goddamn subprime mortgages are still around…."

The connection fizzed, crackled, then blew absolutely clear once more, to the point where I could hear his quick breathing.

"I'm going to ignore that," I said. "Maybe you oughta pop a few of those Xanax you love so much. They do still make those things, don't they?"

"You ever see that Metallica movie?" he said. "What a bunch of pussies! That fucking Hetfield can shove his cross bow up his damn…"

We'd been big fans as kids. When I was 15 I thought the song "Blackened" on their seminal …*And Justice for All* was about Cajun spices on a piece of grilled chicken. "Blackened is the end," Hetfield sang, the song to my mind a sort of humorous take on literary evocations of the Apocalypse, things like Dante and *Paradise Lost*, *Revelation to John*. In Metallica's take, you see, charred Cajun spice on a grilled chicken breast would be our end, the Lord extending a benevolent hand out the clouds to brush the humans down with oil, sprinkle us with spices, throw our heathen souls then into the smoldering sun of purgatory where we'd instantly char a healthy burnt orange. "Color our world blackened." Here here.

When that flick was made, the boys of the prototypical 80s thrash band, they of the black jeans and ripped T-shirts, the overdone headbanger hair, the ceremonial dictators of mosh pits the world over, were fast approaching old age, and though I had not seen the film, in the era of sound bites and free downloads—just post the turn of the century—one did not even need to see movies to get all the presence of nuance and perspective normally reserved for sit-down viewers. Humans had developed so. And yes, I guess I could only have agreed with my brother—the film featuring the aging metalheads going through the motions of a kind of bastardized marriage counseling with psychologists and the like—that the boys were, indeed, nothing but a bunch of wimps.

I lost the signal somewhere in the wilds of the southwest side, between the Western and Pulaski stops, and never called back. The subsequent takeoff and landing were both swift and smooth by turns. Oh! Sweet, sweet Charlotte! How big she had become in my absence! The little knot of skyscrapers so visibly expanding, the hubbub in the airport, throngs of businessmen with briefcases.

My brother met me just outside security. We slipped back through by taking a hallway marked PERSONNEL ONLY and had a beer in the wonderful Meet Me at Cheers Charlotte, a bar with myriad pictures of the actor Ted Danson adorning its walls. The nation was under red alert—soldiers with automatic rifles posed outside the bar's doors.

Leaving, I looked toward one of the soldiers, and written across his left breast was just the single word: "Hanks."

There was a wedding to attend, my brother said. Our cousin was marrying a Naval officer—a strange evening affair on a Wednesday at a Baptist church in the middle of nowhere on the clear other side of Charlotte from where we grew up.

The officer's name was Hank.

My cousin was happy and distant at the post-nuptial reception, a Bible belt classic of barbecued chicken and spare ribs and hashed pork in a "fellowship hall," whose spare design did nothing to encourage "fellowship" of any kind, attendant to the Baptist Church where Hank's brother was minister. No beer in sight. Consequently, my brother and I sat in a corner and sulked. Of this white passel of relatives, only Uncle Jim-Bob (actual name: Wayne) had the courage to meet our eyes. "Well boys!" he hollered. He wore a bright yellow tie with his black suit. He carried a yellow plastic plate, piled high with meat. "Your cousin has done done it," he said, forking a gob of hash. We shrugged, he chewed.

But I love Jim-Bob, I do. An hour or so later he motioned us outside, where sat empty the nuptial chariot (an old bucket of a pristine white '67 Mustang Mr. Hank had fixed up himself over the years into a glistening Southern rocket) covered in paper streamers and with silly foam-written sayings on its windows:

Hank-Honk, just married! Lighting a cigarette, Jim-Bob motioned our solemn shapes around the corner of the fellowship hall into a small stand of trees. He pulled from some hidden place in his jacket a glistening chrome flask. "You boys looked like you needed a little cheering up," he said.

God bless you, Jim-Bob. God bless you.

He poured liberally into our Pepsis.

Go Hank! we screamed, when finally the bride and groom roared off in that fine automobile. We raised our plastic cups and winked at Uncle Jim-Bob, who then raised his. Our parents eyed the two of us suspiciously, and when we got back to the house they gave me and my brother a damned fine lecture. You could never outgrow the sanctimonious elders of the South.

When Pop found out about my secession party those many years before he'd lectured me on the confused morality of any invocation of the Old South, any mention of it whatsoever, really. He was full of woe at the very fact of his history, his Southern lineage. Such feeling was typical for his generation, lofty and full of high-toned feeling about cultural lineage, which to me is race, I guess, and so we get to the crux of the problem.

"To me, 'Old South,' the very term, means little more than the historical existence of black slaves," he told me. The way he said it, eyes downcast, grave-faced, no grin whatsoever, you could tell he took what he said seriously. He took the Old South seriously. But he, too, would call himself Scots-Irish before he called himself an American.

And he had a new skin color to fear, after all. Like so many white people of little imagination, my father seemed to see all the nation's problems reflected in the glassy dark eyes of the "illegal" light-brown laborers he passed in myriad Charlotte construction sites on the way to work each morning, positively angry so many were here, living their lives, speaking Spanish. I tried to argue with him as best I could, pointing to the whiteness of the site bosses who wanted them here, the explicit racism that is the observation that South Carolina's Mexicans were "better than those in North Carolina," as he put it, who were drunk drivers—"They've killed three or four people in the past month," he said—prone to laziness, tardiness and thievery.

Nothing I said could move him from his conviction, and at one point I wondered aloud how a man so very attuned to racial sensitivity w/r/t the descendants of African slaves could hold such a position. "The blacks need our help," he said. "The

Mexicans can just go back to Mexico."

Since 9/11, the libertarian rednecks of the South and their indisputable if misguided individualism had been undergoing an identity crisis of epic proportions. My favorite among their many bits of armchair wisdom—*It's a free country!*—meant to justify the most reprehensible among their activities, had given way to my father's sort of line-in-the-sand moralizing. It was by God a free country no more.

I'm pretty sensitive about race, too, I guess—I am the man's son, after all—but with a different bent. To me the term "Old South" can only be farcical in nature, lionizing a ridiculously laughable legacy to be denounced with humorous ridicule to the end of time. Racial differences are old hat, bullshit, a mere matter of unwitting training of children in all the wrong ideas, performed by a multitude of dim-witted parents, with consequences rippling throughout our social order. Put most of us in a roomful of South Carolina debutante types and we'd all get called very specific varieties of *scumbag*.

My friend Edwin, for instance. He was in Chicago during the period of the Great Secession on vacation from Cleveland, where he'd moved about the time we both finished college in our hometown. He was one of the few at the commemorative party. He wrote a poem for the occasion, a little out of the ordinary for him. He claimed to have based it on Metallica's "And Justice for All"—the song, not the album. He half-spoke, half-sang it to the small crowd on hand. It made little difference that he was the only black man in attendance—all involved drank in the glorious absurdity of the moment. We were opting out, at least symbolically. We all stank of B.O. and beer, equally. Edwin intoned,

It was the best of times, it was the best of times.
Rich humans were killing other, poorer humans, whose relatives in turn were killing humans so poor they may as well not have existed.
With car bombs.
In the public houses of then-Chicago, the derringer was back in fashion.
With the warplanes of imperial powers.
With improvised cricket bats in biblical cities.
With screwdrivers driven into the brains of the unconscious.
With swords.
Words were out of fashion.
Still, rich men were slandering other rich men high in office buildings.
And the poor were asking each other for a little change on the street.

We were all demurring, of course, being poor.
No one ceased asking.
Follow the money.
People were paranoid. Very, very paranoid.
All money trails lead back to…
Justice was not being done for…
It was the best.

I wondered if he was in South Carolina, back in town for the holiday. It wouldn't be the first time I'd run into him there. I hadn't seen him since his earthquake obsession—at least three years prior. We lost each other outside Las Vegas and, in spite of at least a dozen emails and phone messages I left for him, I hadn't heard from him since.

MY brother and I swung by his place to pick up some cigarettes and along the way made plans to spend at least five hours of each day for the rest of my stay in the only bar in town open most anytime of the day, including Sunday. We were dead serious: this evening we would spend close to eight. A not-so-elaborate front for a cocaine trafficking operation, the Silver Dollar circumvented South Carolina's liquor laws by calling itself a "private club," membership to which seemed contingent normally on only whether or not the man at the door knew you or someone you were with. Today a black guy who was on my baseball team in junior high manned the entrance. Back from Chicago? Indeed. My brother and I talked all night of Chicago and work and New York and anything, anything but family. We drank $1 PBRs until our heads exploded.

And the next morning, we were carted off to the crowded confines of my Grandmother's trailer. Five cousins, four uncles and two aunts, my mother, myself, my brother and Grandma and all packed inside. We all of us were there in the trailer, again, minus my particular cousin and her Hank. And for once, and maybe it was my hangover lending a precious sense of surreality to the day, it felt a little right, family. My one time of the year back home would be high-rollicking fun. Jim-Bob sat on the edge of the couch flanked by two of my younger cousins and his gut bounced as he told a stupid story about a man who bought his 12-year-old daughter a Corvette. Jim-Bob spun the tale wild and high and got us all hopping mad at the man, jealous of his little girl who ! Chrissakes ! couldn't even have driven a Corvette to save her life, much less be said to have deserved to own such an automobile. Turns out, of course, Jim-Bob's talking about a Barbie Corvette and we couldn't be angrier with him, that is until me and my brother broke away from the passel of younger cousins and burst outside for a smoke and a quick nip. Then we were just shy of being in love with old Jim-Bob as he folded his arms across the top of his gut, leaned way back against the railing by the wooden front steps and told a big loose one about a three-legged Bluetick coonhound he knew, back when a kid, that could outrun every dog on the coon hunt. I nearly died laughing.

We held a de facto baby shower for my cousin Liz, who was seven months along and big as a house. I was afraid to ask about the father, who wasn't there. But after she opened the gifts, Liz suggested a game. We found some note cards in a small, ancient desk and passed them out to the 15 or so in attendance. We wrote "fond" childhood memories on the cards. Jim-Bob lamented he'd already given up his Barbie Corvette story as I wrote about my Pop's old version of a bedtime story for me and my brother: it was the classic camping kids' surprise-in-the-bushes tale, the climax leading you to expect danger lurking nearby. *And guess what was rattling the dead leaves behind that old oak!* In my father's version the bear coming to eat the kids alive forever turned out to be none other than Spuds Mackenzie, the Bud Light pitchman of a bull terrier of those days, a "real party animal," as the commercials went. Spuds had pizza and Pepsi for everybody, and he was ready to party. I felt it was pure damn genius—a mix of terror and pop-culture surrealism that no doubt fueled my ultimate sense of so many things, right and wrong, the needs of a good story, respect for beer.

Liz collected the cards, shuffled the deck, then read them out one by one. We all guessed at the author, which proved none too difficult considering his or her name was written on the back of each card and Liz was farsighted—as she read she held each card up close to her eyes to read, giving away the author's name to all.

Her own story was the one in which she met her coming baby's father, who, she said, was a long-haul trucker out on a coast-to-coast run today. They were pupils at the Episcopal Day School in town, sort of pre-K mill for the kids of moderately successful parents. She was on the monkey bars, he on the ground below. "I can see your tushy," he said.

Discounting my own, of course, the best story came from

my Aunt Glenda, who told of her first experience with an African-American. "My mom had hired a cleaning lady for a big family Christmas Party," Liz read from the card. "It wasn't something she normally did. When I saw her coming up our driveway I said, 'Mom, get a bucket of water, cause there's a burnt lady coming up the driveway!'"

As if the outcome were predestined among this passel of Presbyterians, Liz shifted gears at this highest moment of spirits, and they all sprung early Christmas on the boy back from the North. Or most of them did. I never made it home for Yuletide festivities—there was something nice about how Chicago mostly emptied out of everyone I knew around that time and I had the place to myself. I'd stayed for the past eight years, alone, and loved it. But a few years back my grandmother bought me a striped knit shirt I never wore and gave it to me at Thanksgiving. The following year, I got a couple other presents. Last year, I brought a few presents to give out myself, and now, though I'd neglected to bring anything this time around, I got a mother lode of crap.

Aunt Glenda gave me a copy of a Nancy Drew book. "Your mom said you like to read," she said. I turned 33 last year. I also got an old VHS of *Dukes of Hazzard* episodes that, I thought, suited. The older you got, the more videos, a default for the man in his fourth decade. You'll need them, son, trust me, the giver forever seemed to be saying. I think it was Barry Hannah who said there was nothing more lonely, yet more soothingly beautiful, than an old man surviving on saltines afloat in his living room on a worn-out couch with a bunch of videos. I have decided this will, one day, be me.

Back home, my mother and father joined in the giving. "I didn't bring you guys anything," I said, but they shrugged it off. I got a used video-store DVD of *Castaway*, the film, from my father. "Tom Hanks is in it," he said. I sulked and gave him a half-assed version of the evil eye, though I felt bad about it later and made like to apologize. I approached him and he was holding the video at arm's length from his face, eyeing the shot of the full-bearded Hanks that graced the cover. "Hey Pop," I said. And he said, "You know, those church women were right."

"What?" I said.

"The old church ladies were talking about how you looked like Hanks"—he put the *Castaway* cover right in my face—"and they're right. You look just like him! You know we almost named you Hank? Except that your mother wouldn't have it.

She figured you'd grow up mean as hell if we did. So we decided on...."

Me and my brother made the Silver Dollar for the end of this night's party. I cried with an old friend over a lost love. I kissed briefly with another lost love in the women's bathroom, before we got kicked out.

I try to keep up with the demands of my dying body. It gets harder. Last winter, I gained 15 pounds out of sheer laziness. Lately I'd ventured out on a quest to lose that weight. In Chicago, I tread the mill daily down at the Young Men's Christian Association. Young Adolfo, a crew-cut, skinny and short Argentinean, worked the counter at the West Logan Square branch. At my hometown branch, where I trundled that morning after Thanksgiving along with carloads of other well-meaning citizens, it was Hector, a Mexican.

Hector greeted me effusively, then inspecting my card. "Chicago, eh?" he said. I nodded and grinned. He remarked that it appeared as if the dumbbells were getting bigger. I missed the joke, pointed out that, in fact, I was getting smaller. "One-ninety-six to one-eighty-five in under a month," I said, "sweat right off my back." Hector shot me a puzzled look. "No no," he said. "Not you. Look at the man. The devil is in the details," motioning to the television behind the desk. G.W. Bush, as if resurrected, was giving a speech from his Texas ranch about some vague threat of terrorist attack.

I shivered. "You too," I said. "Can you see the horns?"

"Yes," said Hector. He turned a transfixed gaze on the TV.

On my way out, after my customary three miles and two pounds or more of last night's beer now soaking the back of my t-shirt, Hector pulled me aside and rather awkwardly invited me to his going-away party at a Mexican bar by the freeway to Charlotte. He was fast on his way back to his native land to be a father, he said. "It is difficult," he said. He'd married here in the states, but it was a marriage of convenience, he said, for his citizenship, to extend his stay. "But my child is in Mexico," he said, nodding as if I would understand. I wondered aloud what his American sojourn had got him.

"Money," he said.

And a wife, I said, citizenship, experience at the YMCA counter.

This was for the moment unbearable, and as my thinking

sprung quickly toward something resembling that of my father, I shut down. Hector was beaming, happy, absent the President. The TV monitor sat silent and dark. "You should come to the party," he said. "I do not care what you have to do tonight."

I bid him adieu. Good-bye, Hector, good luck in Mexico! Strange places were best avoided, I figured. There was enough strangeness in the familiar, here.

NEAR every jackass I knew in high school was at the Silver Dollar by 5 p.m. for the post-Thanksgiving Friday drink-down, a long-running town tradition and going on a ten-year one for me and my brother. We got there at three. The party lasted well into the morning hours. Having deemed itself a private club, the Dollar left her doors open just as long as she wanted.

Some of the nicer folks were there, too, as rounding the corner from the bathroom to the main bar area I nearly ran straight into none other than Edwin, who couldn't believe his eyes, he said.

"I'm always here at Thanksgiving," I said.

"Yes, but…" He had been thinking of me, he said. The network engineer was lately an increasingly adept seismologist, though I'd heard a bit of that, of course.

"Are you better?" I asked him.

"Are you?" he asked me—he might be a psychologist, too.

In summer 2004, the time of the *Passion*—yes, I refer to the film and subsequent historical period—Edwin stormed into Chicago through fiber-optic cables and into my then increasingly fragile existence, long before I was insurance marketer. I bartended two nights a week, barely enough to make rent. Edwin called to voice an obsession with the dredging of the Cuyahoga River. He told me the dredged channel was quickly approaching the mantle of the ball on which we sit, spinning. He got a reading down there one day on its industrial banks that told him a few things, among the most distressing of which was that the eastern half of the United States was in imminent danger.

"Activity has increased," he said, "the peaks now occurring at a frequency heretofore unseen." *Heretofore.* Edwin would use this word—he was a nerd of the first degree. He said the dredging had created what was essentially a fault, a mini fault separating the west and east sides of the city, and when movement along that fault really began, we were doomed. "And not just you and I," he said. "One will have to be west of the

Mississippi to miss the effects totally." Edwin packed his bags and drove to meet me in Chicago.

In the weeks prior, I had been the recipient of a terrible immobility in the face of visions, of a sort—maybe *premonitions* is the better word—in which I moved to take a seat on a bar stool, or to lean my back against a wall, and said stool or wall was not in fact there, whereupon in the vision I crashed rather nastily on the floor, head splitting on impact with a bottle or the edge of a table or some other sharp surface. The delusions, the attacks, came on without warning and were so sharp, so very real that I felt pulled toward their fulfillment. So pulled and shocked, in fact, that I would nearly collapse at the sublime deja-vu-like feeling of recognition.

The night of the very day of Edwin's midafternoon call, I perched precariously on Halsted Street where it rose to meet Chicago Avenue some 50 feet above the industrial mishmash mantle below. This raised crust shuddered with the movements of any number of heavy-duty vehicles—tractor-trailers, Greyhound buses pulling out of the terminal a half-block down the road. When finally my bus came my heart sank at the sway of the ground beneath me. "Yo man," said the bus driver, and I realized, starting as if remembering a life-threatening bit of intelligence, that I had been standing by the paying machine for a block or more and that a large man in an extremely dirty overcoat was waiting on the steps behind me. I reached out to steady myself on the entry railing.

In 1886 a massive intraplate earthquake pulled the sand out from under the feet of former slave Jarrod Epiktu near Charleston, S.C. Epiktu was reported to have "disappeared" into the soil outside of his shack in Summerville. The sandy ground of the coastal area gave rise to craterlets, sandy-soil counterpart to the cracks in the pavement you'll be familiar with from certain earthquake-centric films, or those you've likely seen if you live on the west coast of the Americas or in the Himalayas, maybe, and into which, if the guesses of later-period scientists are correct, Mr. Epiktu fell. Damage care of the earthquake was subsequently reported in places as distant as Boston, New York and Chicago.

It takes a certain frayed pathos to fully believe in your own predictions—I must have been insane, for instance, to have believed that the bus would get me where I needed to be that night, at work at the corner bar I knew and loved, as premonitions threatened to drive me underground. I must still be crazy to accept the solidity of the ground beneath me, just as Edwin could be comfortable with a maniacal assertion of will, could take that and flee the scene of an impending doom in all earnestness, putting his life in the hands of a likely malfunctioning seismogram picked up care of the demise of a certain tectonic research lab in Jackson, Mich. All night long in the bar I could not get this idea out of my head: it required a certain insanity to go on comfortable in your expectations, eating and drinking and sleeping and taking showers and picking up bread at the bakery around the corner, while every tremor that passed through the southern, street-facing side of the building, by which another city bus line trundled every 20 minutes or so, rang forth in the clatter of glasses on the back bar sending an anticipation through me, I will say, heretofore unknown to my mind. When Edwin arrived near midnight, keys to the little Mini he drove in his hand, he didn't even so much as offer a hello before he said, "All signs point to it. Look at the cultural tenor. The Iraq war. The Mel Gibson film."

Where might we need to be, I said, to avoid the shock?

"West," he said. "Chicago will receive the full wallop." Wallop wasn't a word Edwin used often, nor had I ever known him to be given to even quasi-religious assertion, but here it was. It might have been a red flag, a warning, but I didn't take it. I reached for the back bar to steady myself and missed at first, overcome with a queasy unsteadiness. But I rallied. "I'm in," I said. I was off work the next five days, and after I closed up we drove through the night in Edwin's Mini. We were west of the Mississippi by sunup, but Edwin wasn't stopping. We scarcely talked for three days, driving, stopping for short naps in I-80 rest areas or truckstops, listening intently while awake to whatever local NPR station happened to be getting the best reception at the time. We never heard that which we somehow fully expected, but that put little damper on our minor mob insanity. That is, until we reached San Francisco. I looked up a few friends who'd moved there from Chicago just in time to take jobs that would disappear with the dot.com implosion. They rode with us on the trolley like regular tourists, and though I fully expected Edwin to deliver news at every moment of the impending doom, he dashed the expectation and took his sweet time warming up. As night fell in a park in the Mission and my friends' talk turned to near-ubiquitous tremors they felt—while walking to work, when in their apartments, stopped in traffic in their cars—Edwin produced the little seis-

mogram from the Mini and, finally, began to tell of his decima-
tion-of-the-east-coast-by-earthquake theory. Patronizing glances
shot across the circle, seated neatly as we were around a bag of
40-ounce beers. Wan smiles, all. I could only shrug, before
someone broke the silence by cracking another bottle, gulping
and passing it around.

Before long, we were off, back in the claptrap car and off to
Nevada, Edwin said as he wheeled onto the bay bridge. Was he
convinced of his faulty reasoning? I asked, repeatedly. Let their
skepticism fuel your own, I said. "Sometimes, empirical evidence is bullshit. Look to the manner of collection."

He would not answer. As we drove, he cried.

"I'VE seen the frayed ends of sanity," Edwin said, finally,
pretentiously, as he marched off to the Silver Dollar's bathroom.

"Me too," I called after him. "Wasn't that a Metallica song?"
though I knew it was, from the classic ...*And Justice for All.*
Metallica was about insanity, after all, and more explicitly death.
In their 1980s heyday they sought, however confusedly, to
encapsulate living organisms', man's, inexorable and punishing
route toward death in their hectic, unyieldingly pounding riffs.
Death via war, via insanity and bad choices, via addiction, via
chance in the chaos of human experience: the unfinished business of the bell, which on their second album they left up in
the air, incomplete, but if you got the reference to Donne—
and you'd have to be a Neanderthal not to—the implied finale
was clear. Luck be damned. Time marches on. The shortest
straw is pulled.

That bell tolls for thee.

I followed Edwin into the skuzzy bathroom, the soles of my
shoes sliding along the piss-wet tile. He disappeared into the
only stall. "But are you any better for it all?" I asked.

"Are you?" his voice muffled in that virtual repetition.

"Look," I said, "I don't think I really ever believed."

"You have not seen the frayed ends," he said. "Anyway, I'm
not so entirely convinced anymore myself. I have a job with a
federal research lab. I do it well."

He emerged. "That sounds like a fit," I said.

"It is." He moved to the door.

"You're not washing your hands?"

"Take a look around," he said. "You think it'd make any difference?" The brass handle on the swinging door was busy with fingerprints and God knows what else. "Yeah," I said as he took hold of it and pushed and we marched back into the smoke and the bodies and over to my brother, who knew Edwin going back years, too. "Well, goddamn," was all he said in salutation, though. He was getting on a mighty drunk. And it would only get worse. When finally we all stumbled home the sun was nearly up. I told Edwin he could sleep it off at our parents' place, nearby, where we were headed—he'd driven to the Dollar not expecting to stay past two beers but had long ago obliterated that mark. He was quiet, though, on the way, intently focused on the street as I spouted some of what'd been going through my head since yesterday's Thanksgiving/Christmas/baby shower.

I figured aloud to my brother that we were all just crackers, me and him and my old girlfriends and Jim-Bob and mom and pop and the aunts and uncles and military men at the airport and all those terrorists out there, too, if they're out there. "Even Edwin," I said, "though he probably goes by a different name."

My brother laughed.

Edwin's reverie broke. "Don't include me in your ridiculous bullshit," he said.

"We're not ourselves, not humans," I said. "Who has the time? We're all dodging bullshit 24/7—work, play, bills, love, hate, everything evening out into what a son of a bitch thinks about your shoes, or who you look like." Because, I said, we don't have the memories to call up the historical evidence of our humanity anymore, none of us. We believe whatever we want. Crackers. Animals. Apes. Could my brother even remember being a child? I said. I mean it's Thanksgiving—it's Thanksgiving and for Chrissakes what did we used to do when little white children?

Neither of them laughed. "Last year," my brother said, "we did the same shit we just did." Meaning we went to the bar and stumbled to our childhood home like this and I very well nearly had said the same thing.

I had a damn time of it trying to get our side door open. Somehow it was stuck. And I blazed stout angry at that damn door. I pulled my right foot back like to kick it in, then, when suddenly it flung open and there was poor short mother staring at me. I lost my balance, went falling forward as she stepped up to catch me. I caught her steady shoulder and let my head fall there. She just pulled me to her. "Sorry, mom," I mumbled. "I guess it's the Hank coming out in me."

EDWIN didn't speak the entire route to a motel outside Las Vegas, where our journey ended. He insisted on remaining outdoors—he could feel the pressure under his feet building, he said—so we sat around an ice bucket of beer. "Cheers to the new century," I absurdly offered at one point, but Edwin was too shaken to do anything other than raise a can to his lips and gulp. We basked in the arid silence. At around midnight, drunk through and through, I stumbled across the sandy highway that ran in front of the motel, ambled farther along into the scrub grass of the empty space, where I sat down and fell fast aleep. I dreamt of nothing. When I woke, it was still dark, and a slight tremor erupted in the ground as a tractor-trailer rumbled by. I had a headache of epic proportions, and when I stood up I got dizzy with the pain. When I reached the little room we'd rented Edwin wasn't there. I scanned the parking lot for the Mini and it, too, was gone. The TV in the room buzzed a blue screen over the space and right next to it was a note, conspiratorially left on the lone chair. "Horns," it said. "I've seen them."

Disbelief, contrarianism, misanthropism—they can summon mental energies equal to those hidden within religious thinking in their fervent disregard for evidence, faced with its ultimate lack. The human mind doesn't want to make connections, so it doesn't. Horns lurked in my brain for years to come, even long after the apparent demon's earthly body was being eaten by worms or broken down by whatever industrial toxins were present in the polluted soil at his Texas gravesite. For I would see them, given time, during the broadcast of his acceptance of the honorary title of Director of the Patriotic Protectorate, long after all this. The klieg lights outside the Capitol in Washington accentuated the shadows within the creases in his wrinkled old man's face during the curious nighttime ceremony, telecast to the nation. They created a bright-red sheen on his eyes that, in that moment, splayed as I was on the couch in my professional bachelor's apartment, spoke the fear of absolute evil to my brain. I experienced a moment of paralysis, my legs and arms numb and immobile and even my speech faculty halted, tongue grasping for the ability to cry out in pain at the sight, horns rising from the man's head on the television screen. The world is gone, I thought, the world is drunken, smashed.

I slept through most of Saturday. Edwin was long gone when I woke at five. "He was cordial, articulate," my mother said, "a very nice fellow, he seemed."

I nodded. I ate takeout fried chicken with them in silence, then went back to bed. Sunday morning, they headed out for Sunday school at 10 and my brother called to say we needed to go to the 11 a.m. service. "You know why," he said.

I argued with him a little but acquiesced in the end. My flight out wasn't until four, anyway.

We were late—"Hark the Herald Angels Sing" was the hymn we arrived to, an anticipation of the Christmas season. Walking in through the mostly disused front entrance, hearing it muffled from the vestibule where I used to goof off with girls among the acolyte corps, I felt elated at the familiarity. But entering the sanctuary, its new stained glass windows imparting an air of magical solemnity, the ranks of the pews scarcely a third filled with garden variety humanity—I recognized almost every one of them even from my view of the backs of their heads—I felt less elated, less wound-up or -out. A drab easiness settled over my bones.

I drifted in and out of sleep during the readings from scripture. But then the preacher, a young man (he couldn't have been over 40) I'd never met, delivered what amounted to an uplifting eulogy for the earth in the face of constant war to mark the onset of winter. The sermon consisted of a prayer for the soldiers, a strange kind of meditation on death. At a crucial moment, the wind began to howl, to rush along the exterior of the stained glass, the sound intruding on the service, the preacher adjusting his volume just slightly upward.... "And just as we place our dead into the ground the Lord brings water, brings rain that ! yes ! fills the soil with sustenance for the trees, the grass, the flowers which spring from the dirt to fill our air with beautiful oxygen for our bodies, once more." And as if on cue or as if the man had a weather radar broadcast on mute on a screen beneath the bible undoubtedly in front of him on the pulpit, the skies broke loose and battered the peaked, wood-paneled roof of the sanctuary. An audible gasp burst from the scattered congregation, a small whine even from my brother, beside me on the back pew. The preacher smiled. I closed my eyes and prayed, prayed for Edwin, for my brother, for the saintliness of my great Southern mother and the sins of my father and Hector and for my own sanity, in the end, prayed that my bones would be safe in the ground, someday, my skull preserved for empires distant in time and inscrutable, dead testament to the ultimate justice of life, for all.

AFTER the service three old women who hadn't seen me in 10 years or more literally pinched my cheeks with their stubby old fingers and then set to arguing about who I looked more like, that actor (Hanks, of course) who played Gump or the old Luke Duke fellow. I stood and stared blankly at them as they chortled and whined. They decided, of course, on Gump, and I was forced into a humiliating recitation of "Life is like a box of chocolates," forced into it again and again as the old women turned back and motioned to their friends to come and hear, one of whom had an actual box of chocolates at the ready to give me in honor of my return. My brother stood in back of them the entire time, pointing and laughing like a 12-year-old. I blanked every vestige of emotion from my face. "Life is like a box of chocolates," I said, deadpan, over and over and over. It killed them, I swear. One of the former acolyte girls, whom I'd had sex with in the vestibule once, witnessed the whole thing with her husband, a New York City lawyer. "They're right," she told me. "You look just like him." It was humiliating.

I was back where I started. "Serves you right," my mother told me later, as I complained about it over a post-church lunch of bulbous, glistening pork chops and heaped-up string beans and creamed corn and bread and broccoli casserole. "Humiliation can be atonement," she said. "Part of it, anyway." She smiled, grimly. I didn't argue.

She and my father took me to the airport, where I did not answer when they told me they loved their poor little child. There was a gorgeous blonde standing about four feet away, at the back of the security-check line. "Bye," I said. Both my folks winced like I'd taken a swing at them. I stood behind the blonde and got ready to remove my shoes from my stinking feet and quickly lost any sort of courage I may have had. I turned back to where my folks had been. They were gone.

I was two hours early, so I went back to the well-guarded and famous Meet Me at Cheers Charlotte, the bar with many pictures of the actor Ted Danson adorning its walls. I nodded to Corporal Hanks with his M-16 as I entered, proceeded to down two of the biggest draft beers I've ever seen, 32 ounces of piss-colored, bubbling juice in each. I got into a conversation with the editor of the Florida University student newspaper. She was on her way back to Gainesville and couldn't wait to get away from her small-town North Carolina family. "Me too," I said, "sort of." The conversation died.

Ten minutes later she looked up from her beer and told me I looked like the singer from the band The Killers. I did not respond, for I had absolutely no idea who she was talking about.

After work marketing insurance on Monday, I worked the rattling bar. People were there, as was I. We talked and I poured and we all got drunk in the end. It's doubtful I will ever remember anything that was said, as I don't remember it now. But when I got home and finally unpacked, I do remember I found my box of chocolates, Whitman's, exquisite. I loved that old lady then, I did. I even prayed a small prayer for her as I ate, one after the next. I propped my legs up on my little T.V. stand, popped in *Castaway*, and ate until the box was empty.

Also by Todd Dills:

All Hands On: THE2NDHAND After 10 (2011, edited)
Sons of the Rapture (2006), a novel
All Hands On: A THE2NDHAND Reader (2004, edited)

Born and raised in Rock Hill, S.C., Todd Dills is also the author of the novel *Sons of the Rapture*, and editor of *THE2NDHAND*'s two *All Hands On* (2004 and 2011) anthologies. From THE2NDHAND.com online magazine (founded as a broadsheet in Chicago in the year 2000), he continues to edit and publish new and innovative short fiction. In Nashville, Tenn., he shares a home with his wife, Susannah, and daughter, Thalia.

AFTERWORD

TODD Dills founded the literary broadsheet and website and events-instigator *THE2NDHAND* in Chicago in 2000, though at some point he left that city for Alabama and at some point moved to Nashville, where the institution—if that's the right word—is now based. I represented *THE2NDHAND* in one of the "Literary Gangs of Chicago" readings in 2007, and won the plastic crown of the Literary Death Match in their name in 2009. So I've been associated with both Dills and his press—he blurbed my story collection, we've read together at least twice—for some time, though it's not for the standard conflict-of-interest reasons that I begin this piece with so much autobiography.

Triumph of the Ape makes me think about memoir and memories, about the ideals of community fueling literary activity—the writing and the publishing, the reviewing and the reading, the performances and the conversations, the public and the private events. A central story here is "The Stupidist Manifesto," engaging the themes of the collection as a whole, which are the task of the writer, broadly understood, and the writer's relation to a larger society, or levels—circles, one might say—of society, from the friendly fellow-travelers through various levels of aliens and opponents, culminating, in one way, with the Decider, George W. Bush, a presence here synonymous with war, sure, but mainly with a lack of control, a force which leads to increasing insulated conceptions of the writer's task. The war, for instance: one story has a narrator who has an idea about talking about it, the war, the war as a topic, but the bar is hogged by Young Republicans, and *dialogue*, that utopian ideal, seems futile, absurd and even self-destructive, in the end. This is one representation, too, of that frustratingly unshakable force, the hegemony of the other side—the inside—that recurs throughout this book. "WE ARE OUT HERE," those lesser primates, the Stupidist writers, proclaim. They are outside this restrictive, oppressive world. Or they want, in their petty protests, to pretend to be.

Geography matters here. Think Strom Thurmond versus Chicago's Western Avenue at 3 a.m., or Confederate flags versus ambient Wilco songs. The city, Chicago, is contrasted with those outskirts of civilization, the South, outside versus inside, a world of "crowded drunken apartment parties, dim conversations in dusty barrooms" versus the dirty end of the Dixie Highway, full of fire ants and stupid people—people so stupid they don't even know from barbecue, to use one of Dills' bits of verbal jujitsu, the quintessential urban phrase drawing a distinguishing line here, the cosmopolitan connoisseur sneering at the South on the South's own vinegar-and-sugar terms. As the opening narrator laments, from "back home" in some pit stain of a nonplace: "It's my fault we moved, it is. My job brought us south." But Chicago is "OUT HERE" in contrast to all that vacancy. In the face of a stupid, simian world, the artist embraces stupidity as a cause—or something like that.

I, too, was in Chicago for the snowstorm of New Year's Eve, 1998 turning to 1999. This seems worth mentioning because, again, this book makes me think about memoirs and memories, about community and the task of art, about politics and ideals and place. Class, too: in these pages we see rich-enough white kids heading to Cabrini-Green to buy crack. We see how racist and southern-feeling the city can be, and how hostile, hard, "out to get you" it can come across, too. One story tells the tale of the secession of 2641 N. Spaulding—a short-lived sovereign state, self-declared. "We had a party," the story goes, "attended by all six of my friends in the town at the time plus one (the apartment couldn't hold much more than that, anyway)" while in the cultural background, the IN THERE of everywhere else, "the repeat ascendancy of George W. Bush to the abstract imperial throne approached...." There's a chimp in this story, a chimp at a zoo that looks like Bush and reminds the narrator of plenty of stupid, racist, ugly things, though maybe these things—like the war—remain vague. There's a shared rage, a shared righteousness, a shared enthusiasm, but for what?

> *Since 9/11, the libertarian rednecks of the South and their indisputable if misguided individualism had been undergoing an identity crisis of epic proportions. My favorite among their many bits of armchair wisdom—It's a free* country!*—meant to justify the most reprehensible among their activities, had given way to my father's sort of line-in-the-sand moralizing. It was by God a free country no more,*

we are told, in a bit of embedded political critique, but there isn't much more meat here than there is to another character's declaration that George W Bush is the devil. In lieu of an articulated political stance we have a flinching reaction—a disgust, I think—to that IN THERE and its "repeat ascendancy" in American culture. In the stories here of artist types who have made the Great Migration to that promised urban center, there's a fear—a recognition?—that as they say about the past down south, "The South" didn't actually go anyplace, didn't get left behind. "To me the term 'Old South' can only be farcical in nature, lionizing a ridiculously laughable legacy to be denounced with humorous ridicule to the end of time," muses one narrator. Another derides the "Old South Disneyland" of marble-gargling Faulkner stories. We are told that the very identity to which "we"—writers and readers, the implied community of this book—are radically *other* is them, that our identity therefore depends on that contrast. "Put most of us in a roomful of South Carolina debutante types and we'd all get called very specific varieties of *scumbag*."

The Great Migration is not merely a historical event. It remains a central myth of our nation: from the hostile hopeless wastes of the south to the promising urban centers of the north, from ignorance to culture, from shit to being, from the void to the swirling possibilities and potentials that are Creation. Yes, this land of yours and mine is mapped even onto a mystical narrative, a cosmic quest. "Just get the hell out of here," one broken would-be-but-never-quite-was writer turned community college cog hisses at a character in "The Stupidist Manifesto." Just go. Light out for the concrete territories. Make a self for yourself.

This story also has a writer insist that "*The Stupidist needs not the comforts of home, she draws sustenance from the road,*" but travel makes sense only in relation to some base culture, and that's not barbecue shacks, it's the City. As Dills relays in a moving moment, having described a kind of conversational milieu in Chicago—translation, sharing, reading, discussing—and then being dis-placed, back to "the middle of nowhere east of Tuscaloosa, Ala.," where the story's narrator witnesses a scene that can only make sense in the way it makes sense to *her* because of *who* she is, which is due directly to *where* she has been. The meaning she makes is *Chicago meaning*. For everyone else on Highway 7, it's an annoyance; for our narrator, it is "perfectly pregnant as antecedent to the long slog of the Chicago Stupidists, less a march in the lead of progress as an unhappy accident that just slowed down other, more ultimately successful runs."

While the South might not be good at much, it has a knack for bitter nostalgia. I write this from a particularly noxious little town, where the greened-bronze and bird-shit Confederate memorial stares bravely north, awaiting another act of aggression, and where an editorial in the local newspaper lays out the coming presidential election as "a choice between Satan and God." That's the sort of sentence one sees differently having traveled with Todd Dills, from the roiling possibilities and enthusiasms, random chance and rush and high and all sort of sharp extremes, from the city, in short, to the horrible IN THERE of a country that chaws on the word *freedom* all goddamn day, but has no clue as to what it might mean and why it might matter. A harsh dichotomy, and unfair in a thousand ways, but very much my takeaway from this provocatively titled collection, which reads, as a whole, like a book might if written by a man who finally, reaching the beach, realizes the bits of wreckage half buried in the sand are everything that mattered, the places of dreams and opportunity. The damn dirty apes win, every time you wake up not in Chicago, where there is always, as Dills shows us, something unexpected, new and real. "Across the alley, an open window," and maybe it's a bullet or maybe it's love waiting there, but it's something, not nothing, it's a kind of triumph, not a farce.   —*Spencer Dew, Shreveport, La., September 2012*

This afterword originally appeared in the *decomP* online magazine (decompmag.com). Dew is the author of the *Songs of Insurgency* story collection and the experimental *Mont-Saint-Michel and Chartres* text. At the time of this printing, a novel, "Here Is How It Happens," was due in 2013 from Ampersand.

END